Allawe

Allawe

Fran Hasson

2nd edition

ISBN-13: 978-1483974361
ISBN-10: 1483974367

Library of Congress Control Number: 2012918372

This is a work of fiction. While some of the businesses named are real, the characters, incidents, and dialog are products of the author's imagination and are not to be mistaken as true representations. Any resemblance to actual persons, living or dead, is entirely coincidental.

Dedicated to

Chip and Jeff

My Heroes

Acknowledgments

Allawe, as the title suggests, is a novel produced by "allawe," all of us, together. We have come together from far and near to put this story into a complete package. What fun I have had in the process - made more so - by the input and suggestions of so many of you. I hope I don't leave anyone out, so here goes:

Should I arrange my thanks chronologically, I should have to start with Frank Minni, who actually retrieved the box of ashes from a South Bethany Beach tide line in Delaware after a Nor'easter and brought the little chest to the Rehoboth Beach Writers' Guild Millville *Free Writes*. Like Marla, I was obsessed with the little box and the story began. Frank followed the tale, as interested as I was, in the outcome, and aided with many details and heaps of encouragement.

Many people contributed in between and I suppose the last, but not least, contributor was Gail Widmer, a longtime friend from St. Croix who labored over producing the final cover design. In addition, Gail spread the word about my story and read and edited some of the first versions. She encouraged me the whole way.

The "in-between" list is long and valued, some having small parts, others large, but all essential. Here I will have to go the old "alphabetical order" routine. Thanks to: Barb Donaldson for opening up her home and giving me a place to stay for my final five weeks of information gathering on St. Croix. Thanks to: Ginny Bielman, Denise Ferguson, Tia Fizzano, Olga Grkavac, Patsy "Gypsy" Hirst, Jeff Jankowski, Jeanne Kowalski, Stephanie Martin, *miei cujini* Jim and Carol Miles, Jane Mourer, and the Rehoboth Beach Writers' Guild novel class students for reading, giving technical advice, and commenting on various parts as the novel developed. Thanks to Rosaleen Melone for editing, printing sample copies of the manuscript, and for posing for Gail's cover picture. Thanks to Cheryl Fizzano, Stacey Jankowski, Sheila Kelly-Mead, Sharon Prudoff, and Arlene Latterman for listening and humoring me in my endeavor. Thanks to Leonor Gillette, my "ace saleswoman."

Neither first, last, nor "in-between," thanks to Maribeth Fischer, the heart and soul of the Rehoboth Beach Writers Guild, who guided me through the morass of details, character development, and reality checks as I struggled through the writing process. While I didn't always follow her recommendations, I always appreciated them. Any weaknesses you find in this story are the results of my stubbornness and not listening to my teacher, Maribeth!

The final thanks go to you, the reader. I truly hope you enjoy this, my first attempt at publishing a novel. I have loved writing *Allawe*, and re-living some of the precious moments in the 80's when I lived on St. Croix. I want you to love reading it.

Table of Contents

PART ONE

A Gift from the Sea

She first spotted it while smoothing the coconut oil onto her legs. As she breathed in the tropic scent, she watched the object ride the crest of the oncoming wave. The water washed over it and carried it back out. With the next application of sunscreen to her shoulders, she saw the curious article heading back to the shore. This time it made it a little closer but the receding water took it back out again.

She cupped her hand into a salute against her forehead and squinted at the object, which seemed to be a small box of some sort, washing right in her direction. It was early in the season and the nearest sunbathers were reading their paperbacks or lying in the sand enjoying the return of the warm sun. Two small children raced back and forth building a Gaudi-like castle then protecting it with buckets of water in the surrounding moat. No one else seemed to be following the course the object was taking. It looked to be heading directly to Marla, like a carrier pigeon bearing an important message.

"Well, I'm sure not going into the water to grab it," she said to a curious sea gull, who was also watching the approaching box with interest, perhaps assessing it as something to eat.

"What?" muttered Vern, half asleep next to her on the blanket. "Grab what?"

"Look at that little box out there," she said. Marla was not one for going into the ocean. Her fear of sharks, which had never attacked anyone on the Delaware beach, fear of jellyfish, which were seldom in these waters, and her fear of getting caught in a riptide kept her on her blanket or on the sand at all times.

But she was entranced by the little boxlike object and watched the waves bring it in with a gentle swoosh, take it back out, and bring it back until it finally beached itself, riding atop the grating stones and small pieces of shells. Then Marla pushed herself up from her blanket, left the uninterested Vern there where he had fallen into an uneasy slumber, and walked over to the water's edge. She leaned over and picked up the box with both hands, grabbing it before the next gentle wave could carry it back against the whispering line of pebbles and fragments.

The wooden box was big enough to hold four decks of cards, and was mounted on a base that had words carved into the sides. She hesitated before returning to the blanket and looked around to see if anyone had noticed her retrieving it. She turned the box in her hands to read the words. They seemed to be a riddle. *Allawe* was carved into one side, *My peace*, on another, *Sorry* on the third side, and *Irie* on the fourth. She ran her fingers across the words, absorbing them as a blind person reading a Braille museum plaque. They spoke to her, the words telling her this was a very special little chest.

The lid had a milky finish, the varnish having become waterlogged, and the reddish-brown wood grain showed through. It looked like it should lift open and reminded her of the tiny Lane cedar chests manufacturers gave graduating seniors when her mother was a high school student, but this lid was glued completely onto the skillfully-crafted box. She went back to the blanket, cutting her eyes toward the other sunbathers. Still no one was watching her; they were all dozing or reading, except for the rambunctious children, who were now drowning the castle and beginning to re-build.

She settled into the shaded area under the umbrella. Vern began to snore softly. She thought about nudging him and making him examine this treasure with her, but Vern always had all the answers. This was a mystery that she wanted to figure out herself.

The box was heavy but clearly not a solid cube. She tried again to lift the lid, but it would not budge and had no visible hinges. In some spots, the varnish had totally peeled away, exposing the natural wood's rich reddish-brown color. It had been darkened by the exposure to the water, probably from being adrift a while. But how long? The little sea-going vessel had been sanded and smoothed by a true artisan. No rough edges, just smooth transitions at all corners. The mitered sides of the box fit perfectly, articulating into a tight seal. Marla turned the container upside down and saw fragments of tiny felt circles at each corner, barnacles nestling around one of the fragments.

"Damn flies!" said Vern, as he turned and swatted with one easy motion. He sat upright and reached for the Cutter's insect repellent. Slathering it on, he groaned again. "Damn it! This is sunscreen!"

"Hmmm, pretty funny; that's exactly what the bottle says," Marla answered and tossed him the correct bottle.

He scowled at her sarcasm but was attracted to the mystery box. "Is that the thing you were watching a while ago?"

"Yeah, what do you think? It looks like a mini-jewelry box, doesn't it?"

"Looks like a fence post cap to me," he said and reached for it with a "gimme" motion as he stood, escaping a persistent green-headed fly.

She reached toward him with the box, her slender body stretching to keep pace with his rising.

Vern swatted the fly with one hand and grasped the box with the other, but his hands were still greasy from the lotion and the little chest fell.

"Look what you've done!" Marla cried as the box bounced onto the blanket with a dull thud, landing on one corner and then onto the sand, the awkward impact jarring the lid off and exposing its contents. She was both upset and surprised that it had actually opened. She reached for it and saw that a plastic bag was wedged inside, full of a finely ground gray powder. What the hell is this? She was shocked at her thought. "Ashes? Somebody's ashes?" Thoughts of both her mother's ashes and Lane graduation chest sprang to her mind.

"OK, problem solved. Time for a dip."

"You're just going to leave it at that?" she asked.

"So somebody gave his father a burial at sea. He probably said before he died, *Scatter my ashes to the wind*, and Zephyr carried him here. End of story."

She hastily put the lid back on and watched Vern jog to the water and plunge right in. She sat with her box and listened to his thrashing and splashing in the waves. Ashes. She thought of her mother. Today was two years ago to the day since her passing. How strange that these ashes had come to her on this anniversary. Although so much had been left unsettled between them, Marla had grown very close to her mother those last months that she had battled breast cancer, and that had given her a measure of peace. Still so much misunderstanding between the two had never been resolved. And never would be.

Again she fingered the words on the base of the cube. Like rubbing a touchstone. This act comforted her as she watched Vern at play in the surf. She thought of his many attitudes toward matters that were important to her: his forgetfulness of birthdays and anniversaries, his ignoring her when she told him about things that happened in her art classes, not helping to pick out gifts for her brothers, who admittedly were a thorn in Vern's side and hers. How had they come together, her with her highly developed sensitivity and him with what appeared to be a lack of feeling? Before they had married, he was seldom effusive. Did she really expect that to change after the wedding day?

The sunlight illuminated her diamond engagement ring. This diamond was as multi-faceted as he was. She had grown to know the many Verns that inhabited that athletic body riding the waves and loved all of them although she didn't like some of them. She loved the funny Vern, the protective Vern, the reasonable Vern. The aloof Vern irritated her, but she supposed the nosy parker Marla irritated him a bit, too.

She picked at the flaking varnish and toyed with the box, brushing the sand out of the crannies in each letter. She knew this little box had come to her for a reason. She also knew Vern, with his computer geek mentality, would see this as pure folly, her interest in these ashes. A box washed up on the beach and that was that. End of story. Vintage Vern.

A black Labrador retriever puppy bounded toward Marla, startling her. The puppy slobbered, licked, and climbed all over her. She fought to hold the box, nearly sacrificing her two-piece bathing suit to the puppy's affections.

"Bessie, come back here!" An embarrassed dogwalker snapped a leash onto the wiggling puppy's collar and pulled her away. "Her first trip to the beach - mine, too. I didn't think there would be anyone here at this time of the year. Are you OK?"

Seeing the attack, Vern came dripping back to the blanket. He tousled the puppy's head and the two men talked about the beach rule that no dogs were allowed. Assured that Marla was uninjured, he allowed that clearly an exception could be made for this lively puppy. Marla wiped herself down and threw the towel up to Vern. Scratch marks popped up on her pale belly, but no skin was broken. The two children nearby abandoned their sandcastle and toddled, squealing in laughter, over to the wriggling dog, who delighted in the attention.

Marla looked at her watch and decided they'd had enough of the beach for the day. They had planned to go to the movies that night and she needed time to freshen up after the puppy encounter. She settled her Agatha Raisin book, their water bottles, sunscreen, and box of ashes into the quilted bag her mother had made for her, one of the last projects she had completed.

"You're not taking that box home, are you?" Vern gathered the blanket, towels, and umbrella and watched the dog conference move toward the children's blanket.

"You don't expect me to just leave it here, do you?"

"Well, yeah."

"Vern, I'm taking it. It won't take much space and I need to find out more about it." She wrapped her beach robe around her, settled her straw hat, perched the sunglasses on her nose, and headed for the dune. The wind blew her hat off almost immediately and Vern retrieved it for her.

"Where did that blast of wind come from? Maybe another box will blow in. Don't you want to wait around?"

Marla gave him the look of disapproval that he called her teacher-look. They both slipped on their flip-flops and toted everything to the car.

Seacrets

Marla had seen the word Irie in Ocean City, Maryland. Seacrets, a popular nightclub/restaurant used that word for the call letters for its radio station and posted the letters high on a receiving tower at their site. "Jamaica USA," they called themselves. They flew the American flag, pirate flags, and the Jamaican flag around the tower, visible above the other surrounding buildings. Marla began her search there.

"Oh yeah," Johnny Bates told her, "*Irie*, that's a common word in the West Indies – Jamaica, the British and the US Virgin Islands, all the islands where you find Rastafarians." Johnny, an announcer for the close-circuited station sponsored by Seacrets, had attended some of the same classes at University of Delaware with Marla.

They were sitting under the imported palms and drinking Pain in de Asses, a house specialty at the popular novelty club, layering rum runners with piña coladas. Marla looked out across the man-made coral wall that separated the bar and grill area from the beach and shallow water where patrons drank and relaxed in circular floats. Seacrets was a "must see" for tourists. The high tables sat under cabana roofs thatched with palm fronds. The entire complex presented an island motif: restrooms labeled "Mon" for the men, "Womon" for the women, the staff clad in colorful flowered shirts and dresses, and "Peace Police" patrolling the grounds. Their T-shirts reminded Marla of the "My Peace" on the chest. Jerk chicken and other Caribbean culinary treats were popular on the menu.

"Listen to the reggae singers we have here and listen to Bob Marley. You'll hear it a lot. *Irie* is a good word in the Caribbean." Johnny turned the box around and read all four inscribed words. "*Allawe* and *My peace?* No pun intended but *Sorry*, can't say I know about them."

The Crematory Vault

Marla was an art teacher at Indian River and had the summer free. She worked nearly every day trying to track down the origin of the little four by six inch box. Besides the trips to Seacrets, she ferreted from the computer its proper name, crematory vault, as she looked for details about disposal of ashes. She almost told Vern at dinner about the various types of containers for ashes, but the discussion at the meal centered around Vern's upcoming office trip. Several of the men were going to a baseball game on the following Saturday and he was clearing it with her. He was an ardent Phillies fan and didn't often have many opportunities to attend games. They checked their calendars and found that Marla was going to a concert at Rehoboth Beach with her teaching partner, Sybil, on that night.

After dinner she cleaned up and he headed right for the computer, which he normally did. She thought about some of her colleagues at school and how their husbands always helped with the dishes. Some days the chatter around the teacher's lounge lunch table made her want to scream, *But my husband's a great lover! Is yours?* Sybil's husband even helped with the laundry and several nights a week with the cooking. What did she and Vern have in common?

She heard the hum of the computer and familiar booting up *dingdongdingdong*. As she scoured the frying pan, she wondered, How did they complement each other? They both liked mystery novels, seafood, walking on the beach, and going to the movies. Because they lived in a townhouse, they didn't do any gardening or yardwork together. Marla tended the tiny patch of flowers at the base of the front steps by herself. He had no siblings, and her brothers were troublemakers, in and out of the law. His out-laws, he called them. His parents lived in Florida, where they had retired. Her mother was gone, and her father – that was a subject they didn't touch on, so there were no family traditions they shared. In some respects they lived parallel lives, she thought, as she pushed the button to start the dishwasher. They shared the same living space but not the rich life they had enjoyed when they dated and in the first years of their marriage. Marla watched the pair of cardinals feeding at the rail on her deck and realized she and Vern had grown apart and distant, more so since her mother's death, that the red duo outside showed more togetherness than they.

He had rallied to her side during her mother's sickness and immediately after she died, but that had given way to the reserved lifestyle they had fallen into. There was the twice a week sex, the murmured morning conversation, peck on the cheek goodbye, dinner together each night, occasional dinners out with old friends, and friendly, often humorous exchanges between them. They were like an old married couple, familiar with each other but lacking hot passion and a sense of adventure. She wondered if they could ever recapture the excitement they'd enjoyed.

Marla stood in the doorway of the den and pushed her hair back behind her ears as if that would make them both hear each other better. Then she dried her hands, running them down the sides of her jeans. Her engagement ring turned, sliding in the wetness, catching on a pocket. She remembered the night he gave the ring to her and the thought reminded her of how much she missed connecting to Vern in every sense of the word. Before she could say anything, he turned from his seat at the computer, hearing her footsteps come closer.

"Cremains?" Vern must have found the

information on the cache when he was searching Yahoo for a report on Championship Phillies' teams. "You're still hung up on that box? What were you doing, looking for Ashguy's name in the white pages?" He alternated between calling the ashes Ashguy and Ashman.

"Actually I found out something interesting – the box is called a crematory vault." She approached him from the doorway and leaned against the back of his chair. "Yeah, Vern, I want to find more about it." She hoped the discussion of the box would be a shared event, a topic they could use to re-connect and she waited for him to say more. Instead, they listened together to the latest interview on the computer with the Phillies' manager.

But engrossed in his baseball report, he only vaguely replied, "Whatever," moving the mouse over the speaker, pumping up the volume, and leaning closer to the monitor, away from Marla.

Allawe (Ah-la-we)

She had placed the box in the den, to the right of where Vern sat each day at his computer. It sat between two lighthouses and a dish full of sea glass, mostly pieces she had bought rather than found in the Fenwick Island sand. Summer vacation always provided her with time to do things she didn't do as often as she felt she should, like dusting her many knickknacks. She picked the little chest up one day to wipe it and held it a little longer than usual. She stroked furniture polish on it, rubbed it in lovingly, and mused, Maybe a genie will pop up. As she placed it in its spot, she talked to the box. "Who are you, and where did you come from?" Her cat, Molière, sprang up to the shelf and pushed the box aside with one paw. He inserted himself between her and the box and rubbed against her arm, purring and demanding attention. "OK, Mo, I get your message. I guess I'm getting a little crazy over this. Did Vern send you?" She scooped the white longhaired cat from the shelf, and hugged and petted him into the living room.

As she brushed cathair off her jeans, she thought

about what Vern's reaction would be if Mo were able to tell on her. He'd call her friend Ellen or someone and alert them to this growing---what he'd consider---sickness. He threw the term "sick" around regarding just about everything he didn't understand or disapproved of. The neighbor across the street who fed the squirrels on her back porch was "sick;" Ellen was "sick" because she didn't go out on Friday nights; his boss was "sick" because he was engaged three times but never married. He wouldn't understand. *She* didn't understand why the box intrigued her. So she kept Vern out of it.

Marla found a woodworker, Barney Foster, in the yellow pages, who determined that the type of wood was mahogany, a tree common in the West Indies. He knew of a shop in the US Virgin Islands called Mahogany Leap, where many objects were made from that species. One of Barney's apprentices had come from St. Croix. The boy, Mervyn, had grown up sweeping the floor, working the lathe, and doing some carving at the Leap. When his family moved North from the Virgin Islands, Mervyn's mother had seen the woodworker's handiwork at the Bethany Beach Craft show and arranged a deal with Barney.

"I wonder if he went to my school," said Marla.

"Maybe I was his teacher."

"I doubt that. He would be about your age now. If anything, you went to Indian River *with* him. I sure hated when he graduated from your school, back in the day, and moved away. Mervyn had talent." Barney pulled an oily rag from a shelf and wiped it over the entire box.

Marla sat on the edge of a table in his cluttered shop, which was actually his garage turned into a workshop. She didn't know of any other craftsmen in lower Delaware, but Barney was the go-to guy if a parent wanted a wooden toybox or a sea lover wanted an authentic miniature lighthouse. His specialty was replicas of the Fenwick Island lighthouse. Marla had remembered Barney coming to her high school one time during career week. She was relieved when she found his name in the Yellow Pages.

Barney walked over to the window and held the box up to the light. He turned it, inspecting it from every angle, and stopped at the fourth word on the base. " *Allawe* means 'all of us.' Mervyn used that expression a lot." Barney polished the carvings on the box while they talked. "I can restore this for you, if you want."

She thought about his offer but declined. "No,

thanks." He handed the box to her and she traced the letters. "What I'd really like you to do is tell me whose ashes these are! Do you think they could have come here from St. Croix, from Mervyn's homeland?"

"Possible. Anything is possible. This box was in the water a long time; that's evident. These barnacles tell me that." He scraped at the tiny patch that had formed around the bottom. "This looks to be a tiny piece of coral embedded in this barnacle." He prodded it with a pick and dislodged the yellow fragment. "It could have followed the Gulf Stream like the trading ships did in the 1600's. They only used wind power but made it from Portugal to Barbados to Virginia. Little thing like this could easily have bobbed its way here."

Barney wiped the oil on his leather apron and scraped a spot clear on the table for his next project, a breadbox hewn from an area tulip tree that needed to be sanded. "I'm a betting man. I wouldn't wager too much that you could find the owner. It also could have come from North Carolina, Florida, Barbados, anywhere. One thing's sure – it's been on a pretty long voyage."

Ellen

Now with a starting point, Marla developed her plan to discover the origin of the mahogany box. She drove to her friend's tourist agency in Rehoboth and plopped two cups of coffee and a bag of Dunkin' Donuts on her orderly desk. "Here, a peace offering. We haven't seen each other for about a month now," Marla said.

She could never figure out why they had remained such good friends for so long as she shared the notion with many that a clean desk symbolizes a sick mind. Her own artist's way of life was a contradiction to Ellen's. Marla's car was like Marla's dining room table was like Marla's purse. She had to dig through everything to find what she needed, but her mind was sharp enough that she knew which pile everything was in and roughly where her keys were. She had shared that with her mother. She looked at Ellen's desk and thought how her mother would have raved over the immaculate workspace, the tidy IN and OUT baskets at the front edge and the Penn State mug with pens at the ready. She remembered the time her mother had scolded her for her messy desk. "How do you get such good grades? I can't believe you can ever find your homework." "But Mommy, how do you ever get all your papers back to your students? I've seen *your* desk!" This exchange was normal for them. They'd go toe to toe at times. Usually it was with good humor, she reflected, but sometimes not.

"I want to set up a vacation for me and Vern, for his birthday." Marla sat across from Ellen and opened the donut bag, sprinkling powdered sugar as she brought the Vanilla Kreme to her mouth. "His birthday is July 30. Can you make it work? I want to go to St. Croix in the Virgin Islands."

Ellen took a napkin from the donut bag and walked over to the water cooler where she doused it. Before sitting down, she wiped the powdered sugar away, dried the spot, and then took out a cake donut for herself. "But Marla, you hate the water. Why St. Croix? The main attractions are sunbathing and sailing, which you have here; floating in the sea, which you won't do and shopping, which you have at the Outlets right here in Rehoboth!"

"And scuba diving. Remember, Ellen, this is for Vern."

Ellen walked over to the shelf of brochures and flipped through them, pulling out the Caribbean Adventures brochure and walked back to her desk.

Marla fidgeted, pushed her cuticles back, closed the donut bag, got up and threw away the plastic lids and stirrers. She sat back down across from Ellen. "I'll be glad to set it all up, but Marla, I've known you for too long to think you're taking a trip like this just for Vern's birthday. You hate flying and you hate the water, especially water where sharks are known to dine. What's really up?"

"Well, I found these ashes in a little box and I'm trying to track them down."

"Ashes? You mean like people's ashes?"

"No, ashes from a bonfire on the beach." Marla tossed her head and continued with the discovery and what she had found out from Johnny Bates, the internet, and the woodworker. She confessed that she hadn't told Vern about the vacation and her fact-finding mission that she wanted to pursue on the island.

Ellen pushed back from her desk and blotted her lips together, holding them in the tight position. She inhaled sharply and let the breath out slowly. "Marla, this is going to backfire, bigtime. Don't forget, I'm the one who introduced you two." Marla and Ellen had been friends since eighth grade. Ellen had been her maid of honor. "Of course I don't know Vern the way you do, but I'm sure he'll see this as treason, to put it heavily! You can't hold this back. You have to let him know why you're going on this trip."

"But he'll think I'm overreacting like he always does."

"Well, are you? What makes you think you'll find the owner two thousand miles away?" She spread her hands toward Marla, her numerous bracelets clanging with the thrusting motion. "Marla, get a grip."

"It's just a feeling I have," Marla weakly admitted. She avoided Ellen's gaze and dropped her head. How could she really explain the link she had made between these ashes and those of her mother? Their appearance on the anniversary of her mother's death. She knew Ellen and Vern would both think she'd lost it, that this was early Alzheimer's, that it was completely out of the realm of normal. Nevertheless, the feeling that she had to find the owner was as strong and constant as the waves from the ocean. It had become her calling. She *had* to return those ashes to their owner.

"You with all the feelings and Vern with zero feelings. Recipe for divorce court, if you ask me, but if this is what you want, I'll arrange it."

"I wouldn't say Vern has zero feelings." Marla

was abashed at the picture Ellen had of her husband. Tears welled up in her eyes, as they always did when she was embarrassed, angry, happy, anything that betrayed her emotions. She clutched herself, arms folded in front of her. She wished Moliére was there to be hugged. At the same time, she wondered if Ellen was right. Was she pushing the envelope on this, knowing how Vern would be so set against such a mission? Would he be right? She wondered if this was a rite of passage for her, a challenge to Vern's opinion and dominance in their relationship. Was she finally growing up and asserting herself at the ripe age of thirty-three?

The only sound in the office was the tapping of the computer keys. Ellen entered all the data and printed out what she needed for the trip. "OK, as soon as the tickets are confirmed, I'll give you a call, but you should be set for July 23 until the 31st. Good luck with this whole thing."

Marla didn't see Ellen shake her head back and forth as she left the building, nor did she hear the disapproving *tsk, tsk*. She thought back to the summer when Ellen had introduced the two. Vern Alexander was a bronzed mass of muscle squeezed into his red regulation trunks sitting on the lifeguard stand at Bethany Beach, and Marla was a summer waitress there after her junior year at U Del. They were a striking couple, his blonde hair bleached white from the sun, her dark brown hair glistening, both good looking and vibrant, but Marla sometimes thought Ellen had wanted someone more sensitive for her. Obviously, Ellen considered him handsome and charming but a bit vain and unaware of Marla's needs. Here they were after ten years of marriage and Ellen was predicting major problems? Even divorce? I don't think so, Marla thought.

She drove south on Coastal Highway, Ellen's remarks still gnawing at her. Her sunglasses weren't strong enough to stop the sun's glare, and she tugged at the visor, snapping off her middle fingernail in the process. The little Corolla swerved to the right as she sucked her finger. "Where'd ya get your license?" an irate driver screamed at her as he blasted his horn. She flipped him the bird, sliding her middle finger as though she was adjusting her sunglasses. She turned toward him to see if he got the message. Vern, with his impatient nature, would never act like that bully on the highway, she thought. He's not a bad guy. But will I turn him into one with this ruse? Marla determined to tell Vern that very night.

But day after day passed and Marla never found the right time to tell Vern. She questioned her reticence. What did she think Vern would do? Her childhood was catching up with her. She thought excluding her father from her life had settled her dealings with him and his deplorable behavior. Exclamation points stormed into her mind when she thought of him "Stop that stupid noise! That's not music! Put that down right now! You're just like your mother, Miss Clumsy!" He was a contradiction. Everyone who didn't live with him had thought he was the ideal father, the perfect husband.

But she thought of him as a song she didn't know. Five years ago there had been a music in-service workshop at school where the class had to compare significant people in one's life to music genres. She was show tunes, Vern jazz, her mother classical, and her father gangsta rap. No words came to his discordant music other than the exclamations, some as obscene as the ones in those songs. Her brothers had gone to live with him after their parents divorced, and she with her mother. A cruel twist of fate that he should outlive her mother. In any event, he was dead to her. Or was he? Was it his reaction to the quest that she was predicting, not Vern's?

A Caribbean Vacation

The following week, Vern picked up the oversized envelope Marla had elaborately set up on the kitchen table for him. It was propped against the morning newspaper, so he'd have to touch it to get to his sports pages. On the envelope, she had drawn caricatures for each letter in his name with a note saying "Read this first! Before the Phillies' scores!"

She watched from the kitchen sink while his puzzled expression made her think he might go to the Phillies' score first, but he opened the envelope. Inside, he discovered a birthday card, a confirmed reservation sheet from Alpha Tours, and tourist brochures from the Virgin Islands. "What's this?" he asked as Marla removed the cat from the sink and hugged him close in case she needed comforting. She relaxed when she saw the delight in his eyes.

"I thought maybe you'd like to get in a little scuba diving and guzzle some of that Cruzan Gold Rum you're always raving about. They bottle it right there on St. Croix." She smiled. "After all, you don't turn thirty-five every year. Soon you'll be too old for these things."

She thought he might respond to the ageist remark, but he said, "Well, that'd be great if I weren't a working man. What makes you think Darryl will approve this? I don't think I can get that much time off right now."

"Already handled it," she said. Her chin tilted upward a little the way it always did when she was proud of herself. "I cleared it with Darryl before I even made the reservations. Plus, I bought a new two-piece suit at the outlets and a new Speedo for you. We'll throw in a few changes of clothes and head for the airport right after you finish work next Friday." She hid her smile behind the cat's head when Vern's mouth gaped at the word Speedo. "Don't worry, they're swim trunks not wienie benders." They both laughed.

Marla loved Vern's sense of humor. Even if he failed the Mr. Right test in some categories, they could always laugh together. That made up for a lot.

He examined the documents and his eyebrows furrowed into a deepening V. He looked over at Marla and said, "This is awfully sudden. Where is the money coming from? This has to cost a fortune."

"It's not exactly the tourist season there. Ellen

said this is the cheapest time of the year to go to the Caribbean. It costs about the same as skiing in the Poconos." She ignored the "this is awfully sudden" part.

Vern seemed a little puzzled by the surprise Marla had planned. He examined the package again and held up an envelope. "There are two tickets. You're going with me? We always have to drive or take the train and now you're flying?" He stared intensely at her. "Is there something I need to know?" His worried brow touched her heart and she wanted to confess all but couldn't take the chance he'd want to cancel out on the whole trip.

"Like I said before – you don't turn thirty-five every year."

That seemed to satisfy him. Vern dimpled his cheek and said, "OK, St. Croix here we come," and turned to the sports pages as Marla brought two freshly-brewed mugs of coffee to the table.

PART TWO

The Roach Coach

The first morning on the island Marla set to work. "I'm going for a run," Vern told her. "Are you starving or can you wait till I get back for breakfast?"

"I think I'll just have a little coffee here and enjoy our patio. Have a good run." This was an opportunity to get right on the case. He disappeared and then a few minutes later re-appeared down the beach, headed in the direction of the golf course as she watched from the patio. She took the box out of her backpack and stepped outside their room. A maid with a cart of linens was stocking shelves in a laundry closet. It was too early for her to be cleaning rooms.

"Good morning, Miss. You up early."

" I always get up early. You know, to get the worm."

The maid frowned and continued piling sheets in the closet. Maybe she doesn't know that expression, thought Marla. She must think I'm crazy. "Actually I'm looking for some help with this box. Do you think you can give me any information about this, Ruthline?"

She had read the nametag on the maid's starched pink dress. The maid frowned at the sudden familiarity but turned away from her cart and gave the box a once-over, folding and stowing at the same time. "Maybe at de Leap they can tell you somet'ing. Looks like somet'ing from there. I come from Barbados, so I don't know who you can ask, but go downtown to the roach coach. Good food and plenty people who knows t'ings like dis box."

"Roach coach?" Marla gasped. "Do they sell roaches there?" Images of crawling bugs and marijuana joints and roach clips played through her head.

Ruthline could not hide her amusement. She shook slightly with laughter before answering. "No, lady. It's a stand with the best food on the island. Not to worry, no roaches there."

"What about the words on the box? Do you think they'll know them?"

"Everybody know dem."

Marla looked toward the round-about at the beach restaurant and saw a runner come from behind a cottage. She nearly dropped the box and quickly excused herself from Ruthline. "I'll talk to you later." It turned out to be a false alarm but she was embarrassed by her abrupt good-bye and backed away toward her room. She knew her face was red and she hadn't had a chance yet to be sunburned.

The maid saw the fear in Marla's eyes and turned back to her chore. "Later," she said as she folded a sheet.

After breakfast, Vern and Marla made their plans for a scuba dive for him and a look around the island for her. They got all the information they needed from the reception desk. Coupled with the information she *didn't* share with him, they drove into town.

She parked the rental car by the Lymin' Inn, an upscale harbor restaurant.

"You're pretty good driving on the wrong side," Vern remarked. It was as if they had entered a foreign country, driving on the left, parking in a lot surrounded by buildings from another time, another place. The influence of many countries was felt here. The seven nations that had ruled these tropical islands had all left their signatures from the clay tile roofs to the stucco, limestone, and coral walls to the arcades that shaded the sidewalks in front of the buildings. Pinks, corals, pale yellows of the buildings combined with the turquoise waters, skies that frequently hosted single and double rainbows, billowing clouds, palm trees reaching up and spreading their branches – it was overwhelming. They stood at the boardwalk and took it in, neither speaking, neither wanting to break the magic spell.

"OK, let's find the dive shop," Vern said and together they walked past the yachts, sailboats, and catamarans that pumped more color into the vivid scene.

They followed the boardwalk past the Lymin' Inn and a small business specializing in larimar jewelry, the color reminiscent of the turquoise sea. Nestled between the jewelry store and an outdoor restaurant was the Dive Shop. Vern nearly skipped when he saw the red flag with the white horizontal stripe signifying that this was a PADI-certified establishment. As they entered, Marla knew that she was no longer an entity to him. He belonged to the divemaster. She smiled at his enthusiasm, a trait they shared, albeit for dissimilar things. His mouth dropped open as he checked out the walls and breathed in the rubber smells of snorkels, fins, goggles, and wetsuits. Vern had brought along his own wetsuit but opted for renting the other needed equipment for the scuba experience. While Vern selected his air tank and other items, Marla rifled through the T-shirt racks. She decided to buy one to swaddle the mahogany box she was carrying in her backpack. She had packed their bags for the flight and had carefully nestled the box between clothing in her bag. Now she was afraid the edges would poke a hole in the pack.

A half hour later, Marla stood at the pier and watched him merge into the group. She could never stop admiring Vern's physique. The wetsuit accentuated his slim hips, little bubble butt, and the long legs with the biker's bulging calves. Vern between the sheets was another endearing feature. She almost called him back but knew that his afternoon scuba diving would free her to snoop around the island.

As soon as the dive boat was laden down with six divers, the divemaster with his crew, and the accompanying tanks, masks, and coolers, they motored slowly out of the harbor. Marla waved until Vern's group was out past the reef, and then she felt her backpack and traced the outline of her mahogany box, now safely nestled in the new *Get Tanked, Go Diving* T-shirt. She would have four hours of uninterrupted sleuthing until Vern would return to the Christiansted harbor.

She walked over to the town center, a busy

crisscrossing where the incoming and outgoing roads of King Street, Company Street, and Hospital Street converged, divided by municipal parking and home to the famous Crucian roach coach. The intersection reminded Marla of a Sicilian parking lot her mother had once described. She had to look in each direction several times before darting from the shops to the food cart. The roach coach was a converted ice cream truck with a canopy that opened up and emitted scents that tempted locals and tourists alike, who followed their noses to the center of the thoroughfare. Cumin, ginger, finger peppers, Scotch Bonnet pepper, and chili and barbecue sauces could be sniffed out from two blocks away.

Marla eagerly joined the small crowd at the food cart and waited her turn to order from the hand-written menu. Beef paté was the specialty of the day. She envisioned Oscar Mayer liverwurst but it was actually a steaming, deep-fried turnover filled with shredded beef simmered in a spicy tomato sauce. The aroma made her mouth water and she watched while the sweating cook served up order after order by himself. He moved quickly between the two deep-fryers and the crowded countertop filled with meats, buns, dough squares, and sauces.

He deftly slapped sandwiches together and fished the sizzling patés from the fryers, landed them on paper plates, and leaned toward the crowd to collect their money. Marla thought of the regulations at the Delaware beach where hands that touched food were not allowed to touch money and shook her head. So much for rules and regulations.

Locals asked him where his partner was, but she couldn't understand the rapidly-spoken mixture of English and patois. It was hard enough to pick out his name, Enrico. It seemed to be an entirely different language, but she could make out a word here and there. A local man removed his baseball cap, mopped his forehead with his long sleeve and said to another, "Sun hot today, m'son." A teenager with a wool cap full of dreadlocks that looked like a red, yellow, and green windsock slapped the arm of an oncoming friend and sang out, "Wha' happenin'?" His friend leaned back from the waist, twisted, and responded in words that escaped her. The two roared in laughter. "Irie!" one exclaimed and they scanted, a Michael Jackson moonwalk move, toward the ferry to the Hotel on the Cay. She knew from Seacrets that the word meant things were good, but hearing it expressed by these two young men gave it an energy that Johnny Bates lacked.

The white tourists stood out from the locals. She wondered if any whites in the crowd lived there. Some were painfully sunburned; all wore shorts or even in some cases, bathing suits. Their RayBans also set them apart from the locals who mostly wore Woolworth "dark-outs" with tiny vinyl blinders at each side of their eyes. She thought of the line "Only mad dogs and Englishmen go out in the sun" as she noticed the bare heads of the tourists and watched the local folks retreat to the shaded spots in the arcades in front of the shops.

Finally, she ordered a paté, which was so hot in temperature and spice, it took her breath away. She needed to pause between bites, so she admired the background while she caught a gulp of air. Behind the roach coach was Steeple House with its white cupola topped by the red spire and rooster weathervane piercing the brilliant blueness of the sky. Ft. Christiaansvern, a relic protector of the harbor from the past, brought out her painter instincts as she mopped up her paper plate with the dough, catching each drop of sauce. The fort was freshly painted in its original creamy yellow hue with chalk white contours, its green shutters and doors forming the perfect highlights for local painters and photo buffs.

"You need a taxi?" a black man standing next to her asked. His partner eyed her backpack and a little shiver caused the last lump of paté to stick in the back of her throat.

She coughed at the sudden question and then swallowed the last of her food. "No, thank you. I have a car." She wondered if her fear came from racial prejudice. The two moved on and approached another prospect, a bare-headed woman, carrying a large shopping bag with the Carnival Cruise Line logo, probably from the cruise ship which was berthed at the other end of the island. Marla studied their faces. She wished she had told Vern why she wanted to come here; he'd be able to deal with these men. Being a woman suddenly made her feel very fragile. One of the few white faces in the crowd, she also considered that her fear pointed out that maybe she was more racist than she believed herself to be.

A Crucian man bumped Marla as he approached the food cart. "Sorry," he said and nodded an apology. His sunglasses with the blinders made it difficult to see his eyes. She wanted to talk to him. He didn't say, "Excuse me," "Pardon me," or "I'm sorry," just the single word "sorry," like that single side of the box. He moved past her and stopped to talk to a woman who held her child's hand. The little boy pressed against his mother's bright yellow skirt and sucked his thumb.

Two of the four words from her mahogany box. All within five minutes. *Irie* and *sorry*. She noted the way these local people said I-reee, accenting the second syllable and sarr-reee, both syllables stressed but a little more on the second. It was not how she thought the printed words would be said. Marla needed to talk to someone. She searched the crowd and spotted the man who had asked about the taxi. She watched carefully as he and his partner worked their way through the intersection and decided their countenances were very pleasant. There were no hard lines, no hooded eyes, no sneers or sidelong glances coming from them. They didn't hound anyone for business, took the "no thanks" from each prospect in stride and moved on. Marla took a deep breath and elbowed her way to them. "Excuse me," she began. "I don't need a ride but maybe you can tell me where I can find a place or a person who might make a box such as this one."

She pulled the box from the backpack, unwrapping it from the T-shirt. Her hands shook slightly as she handed it over. The taller one examined it, peering closely at the incised letters and feeling the smooth edges. He avoided touching the barnacles. "Prob'ly come from Mahogany Leap or from Edrick's place," he said and his partner agreed. "We can take you there."

"No thanks. Remember? I have a car."

"Kyar ain' do you no good when you ain' know where you gyan'," the short one answered.

She gave him a quizzical look and the partner explained. "He said your car won't help you on this island when you don't know where you're going. In other words, there are lots of roads with no markers and no GPS can get you where you need to go." His English was impeccable, slightly British, and she suddenly developed a different respect for the duo. Was this another sign of prejudice? Again, she was a little surprised at herself. She pushed her hair back from her face and wiped sweat onto her new tropicwear shorts, then felt inside one of the many pockets and jiggled her car keys.

"How long will it take to get there?"

After calculating the time it would require and Vern's expected return, Marla decided not to go with the pair but instead to bring Vern into the quest. She admittedly still felt a little trepidation of being alone with the two strange men. Other women in the crowd, at least those who were locals, wore skirts or dresses. Would they think she was an easy mark with her naked legs all white and shapely? She thought of all the *Law and Order* and other crime TV shows where attractive women had been abducted and worse. She arranged to have the men, Owin and Seymour, meet her at the Buccaneer the next day to take them on a guided tour.

The Interloper

She stared into the night. Vern was sleeping soundly inside while she sat on the patio facing the sea. The full moon painted a path from the distant horizon to the gently lapping water, no more than fifty yards from their room. Below she watched two lovers walking the stretch of beach and remembered walking the beach with Vern on moonlit nights in Fenwick Island. She thought of his playfulness, his salty smell and hair, sticky from the sand and ocean spray, remembered their lovemaking on the beach, oblivious to the sand and clamshells under their blanket. A tightness gripped her throat as she yearned for the return of those lost days. Marla felt like a voyeur as the pair below sat in the sand, then disappeared below her range of vision.

She knew what was to come with the lovers just as she knew she would have to reveal to Vern that she had the box with her. He would be irritated that this interloper in their lives had become so intrusive. But she had to see this through. More than ever she wished she had shared this with her husband. He was not her father; he was her *husband.* He wouldn't revile her like her father had, would he?

Vern had simply shaken his head and rolled his eyes when she'd placed the mahogany crematory vault on the shelf in their den. If the box of ashes had been a burial at sea as he had immediately dismissed it, why did it have the tiny felt pieces at the corners? These remaining pieces, still hanging on, had soaked up the sea. She wished she could hold the box to her ear and hear of its travels, learn its secrets.

She thought of her own shrine at home where her mother's ashes sat in the corner of their bedroom in a tiny titanium "keepsake heart," surrounded by fresh roses she placed there regularly. The jabs from the spikes reminded her of the sometimes thorny events in their lives, but the beauty overrode it all. She kept the flowers in a vase her mother had given her, a blue and white Delft piece she had picked up in the Netherlands. Marla wanted to travel the world over as her mother had, but her fear of flying had kept her from trips out of the country. How strange that this little box caused her to take her first flight ever. Whatever the reason, her mother would be happy that her daughter was now traveling.

She slipped quietly into the room and locked the door behind her. As she closed the drape, she saw the outline of the box spotlighted in her backpack by the last beam of the searching moon. Reaching down to stroke its form, she realized that tomorrow she would have to let Vern in on the quest, whether he approved or not.

Island Tour

Marla and Vern hiked up to the reception desk at five minutes to nine. The tour guides said they'd meet them there at nine. They walked around the lobby, looked at all the paintings, checked the menus from the two restaurants in the main building, and surveyed the landscape from the terrace. "Tennis courts," said Vern. "Want to play a few rounds later?" She agreed to it and they checked the details for courts and equipment.

After a half hour of spinning their wheels, Vern had used up all his patience waiting for the duo. He would rather have gone on another dive. "I coulda been half way to the Cane Bay Reef," he complained to Marla. "This tour better be good. No wonder it's billed as a full day tour. We've spent half of it waiting for them to show up."

Marla knew Vern was impatient with so many things. She remembered the time he couldn't find his gym bag and started pulling things from the closet, scattering everything. The time they were stuck on Route 54 during construction. "You'd think they could do this in the off-season," he had hissed as he gripped the wheel. Little things like the browser not responding fast enough, or worse, Comcast not responding at all. No half and half for the coffee. Only blue socks in the drawer when he wanted black ones. She wondered how impatient he would be with her when he found out the box was in the backpack.

She took this line of thought a step farther and speculated about what had attracted her to him. Opposites attract, the old saying went, but shouldn't marry, said one continuation. His brilliance in computer matters impressed her. His assertive way stood in contrast to her wishy-washy approach. If he bought something that didn't work just the way he expected it to, back it would go; whereas, she would consider it her fault, that she didn't know how to use it, and keep it until she either lost the receipt or the warranty expired. She was vulnerable to hurts and slights, especially by her father and brothers, but Vern nearly punched out her father the first night he met him when he warned Vern that he was in for trouble hooking up with "that one." He recognized that the brothers' penchant for meanness had been carefully nurtured by their father and forbade them from coming to their townhouse. He last saw them at her mother's funeral.

This memory brought in a whole new wave of images: strong Vern carrying her mother through their townhouse and propping her in a soft chair so she could see the bay. Gentle Vern turning her mother to ease the pain of bedsores. Tolerant Vern, allowing her mother to spend her last days of hospice in their home. Why did she think he would be angry with her over this box of ashes? *You can't keep this from him.* Ellen's words pinged off every cell in her brain. It had nothing to do with him being unfeeling as Ellen had suggested. It had everything to do with Marla's lack of trust. She sat down, exhausted from the guilt.

Owin and Seymour finally showed up an hour late. She watched Owin saunter to the front desk, flirting immediately with the receptionist. He leaned over the sweeping mahogany counter and greeted her. "Good mornin', Cherise, sweetness. How are you? How's dose lovely chirren dem?"

While Cherise discussed her two young children, Marla slung her backpack over her right shoulder and hurried to Vern, who had already lapsed into a catnap, spent from his impatient pacing. "God Vern, you could fall asleep on a clothesline," she said as she tugged at his arm and coaxed him out of the cushionless rattan chair on the verandah. His legs were propped up on the rail and his hands dangled to the floor. She couldn't imagine anyone sleeping in such a position. "Let's go before they change their mind and leave us here."

She hoped this trip would be worth the wait, but her expectation was grounded in the rainforest part where a quick stop at the Mahogany Leap was part of the tour. The two followed Owin outside, Marla's diamond catching the rising sun's rays. Positioning his sunglasses, Vern stopped short. "You can't be serious," he said to Owin. The light green VW bus was battered and rusty with threadbare tires. As they got closer, Marla could see that part of the rear floor was missing.

"Wha' wrong? Air condition," joked Owin.

Seymour held the back door open and assured the two that this island car was worthy of every offroad experience they could possibly encounter. Lunch was even included, one seat taken up by a huge cooler. Seymour opened it and offered the contents to them. "You just take whatever you want anytime during the trip." The cooler was filled with water, juices, mangoes, and sandwiches of undetermined content. Vern and Marla exchanged glances and considered a liquid diet might not be all that bad since they'd eaten a full breakfast of fruit, waffles, strong coffee and sliced papaya.

Toward the late afternoon, the van made its way through the rainforest, having finished the Whim Greathouse and Cruzan Rum Factory trips. Marla had researched this feature and discovered it was not truly a rainforest, but it was rainforest enough to her. The hanging vines called out to Vern, whose Tarzan yell startled the tour guides. Marla laughed and made Cheeta sounds and poked his ribs. Owin turned and said, "No monkey here. You go to Barbados to find dem. No parrots, either. We had parrots until 'bout twenty year ago. Maurice, he have a parrot at de Leap, but he buy it from a St. Lucian."

The lush vegetation and sturdy mahogany trees intensified Marla's curiosity. Might the box have come right from this forest? Did the owner live near here? Was she getting close to finding answers to her questions? She smoothed her fingers over the corner of the backpack that held the box and worked to contain her excitement.

The van clattered and bumped, on one rut nearly dumping the cooler through the hole. Vern nimbly leapt out of his seat and rescued it. "Did you get a picture of that?" He could see Marla showing pictures of his bum as he bent to save the cooler. She had already made a cd of the Christiansted harbor and town, the grounds around the Buccaneer, their room, and the beach and was now maxxing out the next digital card. She had an extra card, a fact she kept in mind, hoping to take plenty of snapshots at the Leap and wherever it would lead them.

They drove past towering smooth-barked kapok, peeling turpentine, and ubiquitous mahogany trees. Each time Vern spotted hanging ropey vines, suspended sometimes from one hundred-foot high branches, he nudged Marla and brought his curled hand up under his armpit, scratching, and chortling quiet monkey sounds, his face contorting as he did so. She instinctively giggled and then guiltily wished he knew the box was with them. She would tell him when they arrived at the Leap, but she didn't want to ruin his fun just now. He was so relaxed, like the twenty-five year old Vern she married ten years ago.

They poked their heads out the windows and traced the flight of the chattering birds, hoping to spot a fugitive parrot. After all, even in Rehoboth Beach, there were runaway parrots in the wild. Her mother had taken her to a spot along Silver Lake one summer and shown her trees full of the mutant green birds. Why were there none here where they could live year-round? The yellow and gray bananquits darted overhead while white-bellied swifts whirred higher above. Trilling cuckoos competed in the aerial display throughout the forest. A young boy with pencil-thin legs walked along the side of the road, his ebony skin dusty. He carried a branch loaded with five coconuts in one hand and held a short machete in the other. Marla noticed his barefeet and said, "Wow, don't you think he should have shoes on?" and Vern came back with, "Don't you think he shouldn't have a machete on?" Marla gave this a quick thought and wondered if everyone carried machetes around here. Was this a safe place to be?

The van moved on, dodging potholes and fallen branches. Vern threw his arm against her as Owin slammed on the brakes after cresting a small wooden bridge. She managed to stand up and balance herself between her seat and the hole in the floor to catch the picture of a small herd of goats taking their time crossing the road in front of them. Vern shook his head as he watched the tiny herd plod and chew, bleat and investigate, slowly picking their way until they vanished into the tall bush.

They continued on and Marla drank some guava juice from the cooler while Vern downed a bottle of water. They toasted each other. "Ain't we havin' fun?" Vern said. Marla wasn't sure if he was being sarcastic or genuine, and she wondered if he would be happier at home in front of his virtual life on the computer.

"I'm loving it, aren't you?" She held the armrest as she turned to face him squarely. She loved the smells of the rainforest. She loved the size of the ferns and the towering trees, she loved the innumerable shades of dark skin she had seen, she loved the paté from the roach coach, the sugar mills, and she loved Vern more than ever. Her eyes welled with tears and she started to unzip her backpack, to confess her secret.

A dirt road suddenly appeared to their right and Owin turned the wheel sharply, the van careening on two wheels onto it. He stopped when he saw Marla pitch forward, her guava juice splashing onto Seymour. As she righted herself, she spotted the carved sign: Mahogany LEAP. Below the acronym, in smaller letters carved by the familiar hand were the words: Life and Environmental Arts Project.

She clutched her backpack tightly to her chest and knew that the craftsman who had made the sign had also made the box she was carrying. Confession flew from her mind. Excitement and hope replaced the guilt.

Finding the kind of wood the box was made from had been her first clue that it had come from this island. And the carved letters on the sign were a clear signature to her artist's eyes of the same carver of the box. The whorls at the top and bottom of the M in Mahogany were exactly like the whorls in the M of My Peace on her box. Identical twists appeared on the y's. The way the letters flowed together bore the even rhythm of that distinctive hand. It takes one to know one, she thought, an artist recognizing another artist. She felt like she was coming home, that the mystery would soon be solved.

Her excitement grew and then turned into fear as they were greeted by a pack of baying hounds racing toward them. As the van jerked to a halt, Vern held Marla back as he had when the goats had crossed in front of them. "Let's not be too hasty," he warned. Owin and Seymour had no such fear.

Hello, Hendrix!" Seymour stepped out of the van and strode toward the hounds, calling out as he walked. "Come call these dogs off. Hey, Wendell, hey Calypso, hey Quincy, you go now and let us be."

The three lead dogs stopped their charge and approached more slowly but eyed the strangers and sent low growls to Marla and Vern, who remained in the van. The dogs sniffed the air and continued to approach the newcomers, growling and chuffing the whole time. They were all the same dusty color from the churned-up dirt road. One stopped to scratch his ears. Another licked a sore spot, but their eyes were still on the strangers. Vern watched them warily. He kept the door closed and put his sweaty palm on Marla's knee.

Hendrix appeared from the woodshop, slightly hunched, limping as he moved closer. Short and wiry, he was darker than the two guides. The veins on his arms looked like they were made of the ropey vines from the tallest trees. As he came nearer, they could see that wood shavings peppered his close-cropped hair. The dogs grew calm in Hendrix's presence. Vern opened the door and slid out of the van, still holding Marla back, but they must have smelled his residual fear and raced toward him. Vern backed up, his mouth open wide.

"Stop!" shouted Hendrix. At the command, the lead dog skidded in the dirt and the following hounds barreled into him, yelping, legs in a tangle. They nipped at each other and then skulked back to the voice, whining, their tails tucked between their legs.

"Whew! You must have been trained by a professional dog handler," Marla said as she clambered out of the van. She drew close to the man with a grateful smile while Vern followed.

Hendrix lit up at the praise of his command and settled the dogs. Then the muscular little man directed the group to his work area.

From the looks of his workshop, it was obvious he did not spend a lot of time socializing. The building had only two solid walls, the windward side and the back one. Marla tilted her head back to take in these two walls, lined with shelves, towering twelve feet high. Sliding panels could close the shop on occasions when it was necessary. Various machines showed signs of use, unfinished carvings resting on some, waiting to be polished or cut. Wooden barrels like the ones they had seen earlier at the Rum Factory contained scraps of wood.

"We don't waste anything here," explained Hendrix. He pulled a scrap from the barrel and turned it over in his callused hands. "I can make a bananaquit from this piece." He pointed to a small bird the color of his stained palms. "Like that one."

Two long wooden tables were strewn with

scraps, carving tools, machetes, leather stropping belts, and other tools. Cans of Minwax and various wood stains sat on shelves with rags bearing their scent. An antique lathe was by the table, fragments of sandpaper at its feet. Not far from it was an electric lathe. Marla had seen many of these tools in Barney's shop in Delaware. Except for the machetes.

Inside the cavernous shed were hundreds of creations carved or crafted from mahogany by various Crucian artists. Hendrix showed them the stacks of the various woods: rare black teak, flamboyant, dark red lignum vitae, and other native woods. He displayed various pieces he, himself, had made and told them what kind of wood they were carved from. "Here," he held out a cedar mongoose the same color as the bananaquit, "hold it yourself. Maybe you have a child at home who would like this." His tone was a practiced one, probably a sales pitch he had developed over the years. Other than bananaquits and mongoose, among his carvings were palm trees and hibiscus blossoms, knife holders and some bookends that were actually unlathed chunks of wood, polished to a high sheen. One chunk was engraved "Allawe." The lettering was from a different hand, but blood pounded at her temples. She held it out to Vern. "Like my box." He rolled his eyes and she decided this was probably not the time to pull the chest from her backpack. Was there ever going to be a good time? Maybe she would save the conversation for later and come back here tomorrow.

Vern was more interested in the larger items that were done by the various carvers. The two walked away from Hendrix. A planter's chair with elongated arm extensions caught his fancy. "Here's one we should have. Remember in the Whim Greathouse they told us how the man of the house would sit and have his boots pulled off for him? I think I'd like that." He patted the seat of the chair and worked at one of the extensions.

"Yeah, right." Now it was her turn for the eyerolling. She curtseyed to him and then went back to replace the *Allawe* piece to its spot, its outline marked on the shelf by the absence of sawdust when Seymour called Hendrix over and said, "The lady has a box she wants you to look at."

Suddenly the thickness of the air grew and choked her. The pungent, resinous odor of the turpentine trees, sweet fragrance of the mother-in-law tongues, thick sweet orchid smells made their way into the workshop and combined with the sawdust from the mahogany scraps. The density of the air closed in on her as she watched Vern's eyes widen in disbelief and hurt. Her hands trembled as she unzipped her backpack, but she had no choice now except to plunge right in, the way Vern always plunged into the surf at home. Let the waves take her where they may, she thought; she was now in over her head. She didn't look at Vern for fear she might not go through with her brave resolve. His look had surprised her; she had anticipated more anger than hurt. Maybe Ellen had a better understanding of her husband than she did.

He watched wordlessly as she pulled the mahogany box out and held it up for Hendrix's inspection. He turned away and resumed looking at the large items while Marla addressed the carver. Refusing to be part of the process, Vern didn't watch what happened next. Marla saw him run his hands over an altar rail that was a work in progress. He seemed to have lost himself in the altarpiece with its smooth surfaces that gleamed and set off the seven gothic panels. But Marla knew his ears absorbed the conversation of the group. She was aware of him clenching and releasing his fists, taking deep breaths as he re-examined the rail.

She faced Hendrix and in a tremulous voice

asked, "Did you create this box?" Marla held it out.

Hendrix took the box from her, almost reverently, and ran his rough, scarred fingers across the words at its base. The carver closed his eyes and brought it to his face, caressed his face with it, brushed it with his lips. He opened the lid and recoiled when he saw the bag of ashes inside. "Mother of God," he whispered. "Why you have dis box, dese ashes?" His face twisted and he glowered at Marla.

The dogs stirred, and walked stiff-leggedly toward the group. Vern's fear began to emanate from his pores and the hounds, no doubt sensing it, began their low growl again. He quickly doubled back to his post at Marla's side.

Marla was now afraid, too. She had feared Vern's wrath, which she knew she would face when he discovered the real reason behind the "vacation," but she never thought there was something to fear because of possessing the box.

Hendrix closed the box and pushed it toward her as he retreated. His lame leg caused him to lurch as he backed away and Marla nearly lost her grip on the ashes. "Please, let me explain," she said. Her whole body trembled and tears sprang to her eyes. She moved toward him, clutching the box to her breast. The air was being sucked from her and the thick odors of the rainforest again blanketed her. Her eyes and voice were pleading but Hendrix tensed and gritted his teeth, wrenching his body away from her nearness. She felt Vern's hand on her arm and this comforted her.

Seymour nodded toward the carver and held his hand out in a peaceful gesture. He looked like Jesus saying, *Come ye little children.* "They're tryin' to return it to its owner; they mean no disrespec'," he explained.

Hearing the intention spoken in the cadence of his people, Hendrix stopped his backward scrabbling and stood still, but he kept a steady gaze on Marla and the offensive box. Seymour and Owin convinced him she was no she-devil, no goatfoot woman bringing Obeah vengeance upon anyone.

"It's OK, Hendrix. These ashes came to her from Delaware." He paused to see if that registered with the little man. Hendrix's brows furrowed, so Seymour went on. "That's by New York. They washed up on the beach and she wants to see that they get back to their owner. That's all."

Hendrix looked down at Marla's sandaled feet and back up at the box. "Me ain like dis." Agitated, Hendrix mixed patois with English. Marla tried to catch the gist of what he was saying, but it came out garbled. His voice was low with an edge of fear creeping into it. "Edrick, he make de box. He make it for Clemma Joseph over by Mon Bijou." Marla looked toward Seymour for the meaning, but the guide's piercing gaze drilled through her and warned her to not stop him. "Dat's all I say." Hendrix shook his head and folded his arms.

In spite of the warning, Marla timidly asked Seymour, "Where can we find this Edrick?"

Seymour nodded toward Hendrix. "Edrick, he off-island now t'ree year." Marla had a hard time hearing and a harder time understanding. "Ms. Joseph, ain know where she be now. She daughta liv up in Peter's Rest." Hendrix held his hands up to his face, massaged his temples, and spat on the ground. He scowled at Marla. Then surprisingly, he scowled at Seymour and Owin. " Buss off now, ain' like dis business." He turned and limped out of the workshop, the hounds following but glancing back at the offenders and warning them with a *woof* now and then. Hendrix never looked back.

A Moment of Reckoning

On the way back to the van, Seymour explained what Hendrix had said. "There used to be another master carver here, Edrick. He's the one who made the box for Clemma Joseph, from Mon Bijou." She remembered that at the roach coach one of the guides said that it looked like Edrick's work. It had been an immediate response, one reflecting Edrick's fame as a carver. "Mon Bijou," Seymour continued, "that's a section of the island. Her daughter lives in a different section called Peter's Rest."

Marla felt a beam of understanding lighting her eyes. She smiled, proudly remembering having read of some of the fanciful names for parts of St. Croix.

"He didn't know where Ms. Joseph was and Edrick left the island three years ago." He told her Hendrix's last statement meant he wanted nothing to do with her again. "At least I think he only meant you, but he seemed angry enough that he may have meant us, too."

"I don't understand his anger." Marla settled the box into the T-shirt and put the backpack on the seat. I do understand Vern's anger, she thought. She looked at him but felt an invisible pull that jerked his head away from her. "I never meant to offend him." Or you, she wanted to add to Vern.

No one in the car responded. Owin turned the key in the ignition and slowly bumped over the ruts toward Scenic Road to begin the trip back to the hotel. A cloud of dust obscured Mahogany LEAP and Hendrix, but the memory of all that happened was clear as the diamond she wore. She twisted the ring around her finger and couldn't seem to stop the motion. She wondered if their marriage was now in jeopardy. How mad was Vern? She had never before deceived him.

They rode back to the Buccaneer mostly in silence. She could feel Vern bristling, his anger growing with every dip in the road. He would not look at her. She tried to make small talk with the tour guides, asked about a mongoose that scurried across the road like a short-legged squirrel with a straight tail.

"Mongoose king of de day, rat king of de night," Seymour politely told her, but he wasn't very keen on talking to her, either. He gave a little history of the introduction of the mongoose on the island and its impact on the snake population, but the knowledge that she was carrying someone's ashes stifled all attempts. She knew the two Crucian men shared Hendrix's distaste. She understood that in their society, carrying someone's remains about was not correct behavior, but they probably tolerated more from tourists because of the money they were able to extract from their wallets. Marla wasn't one for carrying ashes around, either, but this was clearly an exception. More than once Marla saw Owin look back through the rear-view mirror and then exchange glances with Seymour as they murmured in the West Indian cadence with words she couldn't make out.

"At least we don't have to worry about snakes crawling into our room at night." She thought this would get a rise from Vern. He hated snakes as much as she did, but he maintained his cold posture and didn't respond at all. All this time he just looked out the window as they backtracked to the Buccaneer. And Marla stewed in her own miasma. She thought of all the missed opportunities to bring Vern in on the plan, all the worrying she had done, all the hopes for finding the owner of the ashes. She dropped her head and glanced over at the backpack, wishing the box had washed up in Rehoboth or Miami, anywhere but Fenwick Island. She sighed and slumped back in the seat, feeling defeated.

A young boy ran out from a break in the bush, laughing, his barefeet kicking up the dust. His eyes widened and his expression froze as he saw the van approaching; then he scampered quickly back into the tall grass. As Owin slammed on the brakes, the backpack slid forward and Marla grabbed it before it could bounce toward the hole in the floor. Vern remained silent, sat with his arms folded across his chest, staring out the window, and acted as though nothing had happened. Marla embraced the pack, comforting it like she would have held that child. She renewed her silent pledge to return the ashes. It was a heavier burden than ever but one she knew she had to honor. What if these ashes were of a little boy like that one, she thought.

The golf course finally appeared and Marla was relieved that they were back at the hotel. "Wow, it was way shorter coming back than it was going," she said, again struggling to get some dialogue going. It still didn't work. They passed silently through the gate with a wave at the guard and motored up the winding access road to the reception area. Vern stared straight ahead. The van came to a grinding halt and Owin waited while Seymour escorted the two from the van. Vern paid them the fifty dollars for the tour, muttered a quiet thank you, and headed for their room. He did not look back at Marla.

She watched him. It was a long walk to their room in the wing that sat at the base of the property, on the other side of the hill. The tiki bar and beach waited in that same private cove. She had hoped they could have a late afternoon drink and sit under the palm trees for a while. His silence told her that it wasn't happening. "Your husband was quiet all the way back," Seymour began. "He wasn't happy with the trip?"

"He wasn't--- isn't--- happy with me, but it has nothing to do with the tour. Thank you for your help today. I do want to go to Mon Bijou or Peter's Rest and find Ms Joseph, though. Do you have a card so I can call you when I'm ready to go there?"

Seymour backed off before saying, "Sorry, but me ain' one for dealin' wid no dead folk." His sudden use of local language and pursing of his lips showed her he was finished with these tourists, who were now taboo to him and Owin.

Her eyes teared as she hiked the bag over her

shoulder, clenched her fists and began the lonely walk down the hill to their seaside room. She did not glance up at the billowing clouds racing across the turquoise Caribbean, did not see the palms giving her a royal welcome as she got closer to her room. She wondered if Vern would still speak to her or if he would be packing his bags for an early return home. This was only their third day here and his birthday was five days away. She was both angry and disappointed. Angry at Vern for being angry with her. Angry with herself for designing the entire plot. Angry at the ashes for coming to her. She didn't return the wave as a worker passed her in a golf cart, heading for the main building. Angry at him for interrupting her thoughts. She sat at a bench, placed there for guests to savor the view, but used by her now in this tense moment. She needed to calm down before seeing Vern.

Was her quest going to cause an incurable rift between the two? Was Ellen right? Was this journey a recipe for serious marital problems? Was he so selfish that he couldn't give her this space? He, selfish? She took a deep breath and looked up, finally seeing the beauty around her. What am I thinking? Everything about this has been my selfishness. And self-righteousness. If it had been up to Vern, we'd have left the box on the beach the day it splashed in. Still, she believed she was right to track down the owner. But how would she deal with Vern's anger?

The room was empty, but the bags were all still there, clothes hanging as they had left them, and the only change was that the housekeeping staff had serviced the room. The floral bedspread was straightened, an ice bucket stood sweating on the stand beside the complimentary Cruzan Rum bottle, and the insulated drapes were closed on one window against the tropical sun. At the other door, the heavier drape was pushed aside and the gauzy inside curtain parted as the trade wind blew. Marla saw Vern sitting on the patio. She relaxed a little, shrugged her shoulders and let them go several times as some of the tension flowed out.

He was looking out at the sea and holding a glass in his hand. She heard the rattle of ice and watched him tilt the glass to his lips. She knew he had heard her come in, but he didn't acknowledge her.

She placed her backpack on the bed and removed the box from its protective T-shirt. She carefully set it on the table and poured herself a rum and Coke, and dropped two ice cubes into the drink. She slipped through the inside drape, balancing the mahogany box on her hip and the glass in her hand as she joined Vern on the patio. She settled herself across from him and set the box on the table between the two. "We need to talk," she began.

He continued to look out at the sea and didn't notice her upturned chin or the set of her jaw. "What's to talk about? Looks to me like you've got it all figured out. Hmmm, my birthday vacation." He turned his head toward the ashes, looming large between them. "Yeah, right. It was all about *that*, all along." He still did not meet Marla's eyes.

But she searched his. And saw the hurt, which again surprised her. She had steeled herself against his certain anger with a determination she seldom called up. Now she wasn't sure how to proceed. "I'm sorry. I thought if you knew I was bringing the ashes, you wouldn't come. And it is a special birthday vacation for you as well as a mission for me."

"Mission?" The word burst out. He turned and faced her, his face starting to redden above the sunburn. "Marla, for God's sake. You've been obsessing over this thing for nearly a month now. Every day I see the "vault" when I go into the den. Every night when you do that thing with your mother's heart, I can see you want to bring those fuckin' ashes and put them next to hers. What the hell is going on here?" His voice was reaching a pitch that she had heard only three times in their twelve years together. Once before they married and twice with her brothers. "Will we spend the rest of this so-called vacation climbing coconut trees, swinging from vines, looking for the owner of this God damn box!"

She took a long swallow of the rum drink and breathed deeply before answering. "I hoped you'd understand."

"How?" he asked. "Have you tried to explain anything to me?"

"You've always laughed at this and ignored me when I wanted to bring it up."

"I had no idea what was going through your mind. Don't you think this is really a little crazy, being so obsessed with this?"

"I just know in my heart that box found its way to me, that somehow, like a message in a bottle, those ashes are calling me to return them." Tears welled up and she took another deep breath. " And 'that thing' I do with my mother's heart is pray. Just like I do for these ashes."

Vern's eyes softened and he looked out toward

the sea. "Why all the secrets about this? What's ever happened between us that you couldn't tell me about this? What did you think I'd do?" He searched her face but she bent her head and avoided his eyes. "Do you have any idea how I felt out there with those strangers? Everybody knew you had the box, everybody but me." Their eyes met and flickered, repelling each other; she looked away and back and then he did the same. She could see the anger then the hurt then the anger, back and forth.

She told him how she had come so close to telling him but each time she held back. "I don't know why I couldn't just come out with it."

"Then we have a bigger problem than you finding Ashman. Are we in trouble? Am I such an ogre?" He tilted his head to the side and waited for a response.

She leaned on the table with both elbows, cradling her nose with steepled fingers. Tears began to slide down her cheeks. She sniffled and blew her nose on a cocktail napkin. "Vern, do you know they washed up on the second anniversary of Mother's death?" She tilted her head toward the ashes. "Do you remember I almost had the funeral home put her ashes in her little cedar chest, like this box?"

Her next words were barely audible. "Do you know I'm still not done grieving over her, that I still want to make things right?"

He sharpened his gaze at her and said softly, "Babe. Your mother is gone. You did everything you could to make her last days as pleasant as possible."

"That's just it. I don't mean just those last days. I mean a lifetime of regrets." Now her body shook with sobs. "I'm just so sorry."

Vern got up from his seat and pulled her into his arms. "Go ahead and cry. You have the weight of the world on your shoulders; you care about everybody, everybody but yourself." He kissed the top of her head. "Let me into that world. Please, don't keep any more secrets."

Marla wept into Vern, releasing tears from the tension that had been building, tears from a childhood of hurts, tears of joy that he was holding her, but she wondered if she could suddenly break a lifetime of habits.

Scuba Vacation, Wonderful Wife, and a Ghost

Marla was relieved. Even though she knew he wasn't about to embrace her mission, she knew he would be tolerant, and that her secrets were not a deal breaker. She wanted to call Ellen, to tell her she was wrong about Vern. Instead, she telephoned the front desk and asked for two seats at the terrace for that evening.

The sun had already begun to dip beyond the horizon. To the west, the clouds played with the remaining light, splashing swatches of charcoal and orange across the sky. Marla captured the light show with her camera. "I can use these for paintings when we get home. Look how the colors are changing. Now it's yellow over there." She could feel Vern watching her snap photo after photo. She felt he was more interested in her than the scenery.

She hoped he was not changing his mind about forgiving her. She turned to him and saw that he was relaxed, wearing the Vern smile that was such a comfort to her.

"I'm a lucky man," he said, pulling the block of pineapple off the swizzle stick on his drink. "A scuba vacation and a wonderful wife. Not to mention a ghost." He lifted one eyebrow and continued. "I'm going to try and get in as much scuba diving as I can while you poke around. Is that OK with you?"

Marla didn't want to push her luck, had hoped to have the security of him being with her, after the response at the LEAP, but was happy not to have a total loss of trust over her mission. "Agreed. Will I be allowed to talk to you about it?"

"If you must. Will I be allowed not to be excited?" He tilted his head, hunched his shoulders, and dimpled his cheek.

"If you must not." She met his shrugged shoulders with her own. She held her piña colada up. " *Saluté.*"

That was a start. They enjoyed the jazz trio and dinner and walked back down the hill to their room. Vern watched some Cable TV and Marla, exhausted by all that had happened, fell asleep, her last thoughts that there was still a distance between them. During the night, she awoke and looked over at Vern. Through a gap in the drapes, the moonlight picked out his sleeping face, so peaceful, so completely at rest. The sunburn had already faded to a light tan and his blonde hair shone like gold. She thought about stroking his outstretched arm. But she fought the impulse. Suppose he was too deep in his sleep, or worse, not interested? Perhaps the day's events needed to settle a little.

Rosalie

Vern's dive group would be leaving from the Frederiksted pier after lunch, so the two drove to the opposite end of the island and sunbathed on the white sandy beach before eating at a little vegetarian café at the edge of town.

He hugged Marla before he left her for the dive. "Don't get too worn out. I have plans for tonight." He patted her behind and went off with a knowing look. Her fear the night before about his lack of desire for her was ungrounded. That morning had been better than it had been for the past two years, and Marla felt like the journey had been worth it whatever the outcome of her quest. In fact, as she crossed the street to look for a print for his boss, she wasn't even thinking about Clemma Joseph, Hendrix, or anything related to her search. She remembered Vern's powerful arms, his minty breath on her neck, their passion for each other.

The squeal of brakes and shouts from onlookers brought her up short. A man raced out from the shaded sidewalk and pulled her by the arm to him, the hibiscus she'd stuck in her scrunchie falling to the street. A car brushed her beach cover-up as it swerved past her. The driver didn't stop, just leaned on his horn and continued through town. The Crucian man released his grip and stood back. "Wha' wrong with you? You need to look before crossing."

Marla had forgotten about the driving on the left, so deep was she in her thoughts. Now she shook and watched the car round the corner. A woman joined the two as Marla straightened herself out and regained her composure. "Here, don't lose your pretty flower," the woman said as she handed the bloom to her.

"Thank you. And you, too." She turned to her rescuer. "You saved my life. How can I ever repay you?" As the words came out of her mouth, she realized how trite they sounded, but what else could she say?

The man smiled, and the grey stubble against the dark brown face shone in the bright sunlight, creating a halo around his upturned chin. "No need," he said. "You just be careful from now on." With that he continued his walk down Strand Street, looking back when he reached the corner to see if she was following his directions. Flags of many nations fluttered in the breeze over the hotel where he stood. He waved at Marla before crossing to the shade of the next arcade. A tired dog slowly crept across the street and threw himself down in front of her, its elbows cracking against the cobbled sidewalk. The dog sighed and looked up at her as if to tell her he knew how to cross the street by himself and blankly looked toward the sea.

"That was a close call," she said to the woman. Her voice began to shake as the realization fully hit her. "I think I need to sit down a minute."

"Now don't you be eyeing up those benches over there. Come on into my shop here and have a seat." She took hold of Marla's arm with a gentle touch, but one that possessed authority. "You've had enough crossing the street for now. It almost looks like you've had enough of St. Croix." The woman led Marla inside to the coolness and protection of the artsy gift shop.

Marla felt transported, safe from the burning heat rays, cars driving on the wrong side of the street, tour guides and Hendrix, keeping secrets from Vern.

"I'm Rosalie." The woman extended her tanned hand to Marla, whose pale arms shouted "tourist tourist" despite the days she'd spent with Vern on the beach before coming to the island. Rosalie's tan was more of a permanent variety, deep and healthy, setting off her white teeth and sparkling blue eyes. "Welcome to Frederiksted; you've just seen the best and the worst." She shook her head back and forth as she pointed to the street. "You were almost killed by that devil, Elvin Warner, but our local angel, Willis Kean, came to your aid. That's how it is here sometimes, a real close-up of good versus evil in day-to-day living."

"I'm sure glad the good outweighed the bad." Marla massaged her temples.

"How about a nice chai? It'll relax you and then you'll be ready to go on with what you were doing."

"I'd love a cup." It was such a relief to hear words she could understand. "Where are you from? You don't sound like most of the people I've been talking to."

"I visited from New Jersey about twenty-five years ago on a vacation and I've been here ever since. I opened this shop ten years ago." Rosalie toyed with her string of seeds, gray ones the size of Milk Duds, separated by tiny black ones and bright red mid-size seeds. The seed necklace reminded Marla of rosary beads. And of her mother, a devout Catholic who never got over Marla being married in an Episcopal church. One of their unresolved conflicts. But her mother had lived with it, saying the Episcopalians were just one step down from Catholics. Another source of conflict. In her mother's eyes, Marla was always one step short of perfection in everything she did.

Conflict dogged her. Growing up it had been with her parents. Her father always loomed over her with his abusive remarks. Her mother often ignored her, just as painful. Her brothers taunted her. But she had held her position, even at times when secretly she knew she was wrong. As she thought of the rosary beads and her mother, she wondered if this was one of those untenable moments in time, this quest, this mission to find the ashes' owner.

Rosalie continued, "I really can't imagine living anywhere else now."

"More power to you; I can't believe anybody would stay here that long." She wondered if she'd ever be able to understand the local dialect and speech and if her tour guides would tell the whole island she carried a dead person around with her. "It's a beautiful place, to be sure. I hope I'm not being rude, but what kept you here?" Marla stretched her legs and leaned back in the caned seat, her arms resting on the jade taffeta pillows fluffed against each wooden arm. She noticed the extensions recessed in the arms and laughed. "Is this a planter's chair?" It was like the one Vern had admired at the LEAP. She was delighted as Rosalie pulled the extensions out and told her to put her legs up while she went for the chai.

"I stayed here because of little goodies like that chair," Rosalie called out as she retreated behind heavy flowered drapes that separated the showroom from her private quarters.

Marla stretched her legs out, drew them back, fluffed the pillows, and considered zoning out for a short nap. But as she surveyed the shop, her energy rebounded. Her eyes devoured the watercolors hanging on the wall opposite her. Local artists had captured the bright rainbows, shades of Caribbean blue, galvanized shacks hidden between stalks of cane and tall reeds. She hefted her legs from the extensions and swept herself to the wall of paintings. The louvered windows were tilted so the sun's rays were diffused and they cast a soft illumination on the varied articles in the store: bright batik wraps to the right of the planter's chair, original greeting cards on a rack next to them, a tasseled ottoman for weary tourists by the cash register. To the side of the drapes were stacks of air-brushed T-shirts with sailboats, sugar mills, palm trees standing guard over white beaches, the many sights of St. Croix.

Marla returned to the prints and considered what Darryl might like. She was grateful to Vern's boss for allowing this trip on such short notice. She wanted to select just the right one for him. As she absorbed the peaceful settings in the prints, she swayed a little, savored the memory of Vern's touch, opened her heart to all the good that had happened. She thought of the little box sitting back in the hotel and voiced a silent prayer of thanks. She decided on a street scene of Frederiksted, complete with a dumpster dog and historic banyan tree, a corner of the painting revealing the turquoise sea, multi-colored crotons, and palm fronds. Darryl would love it.

Once she'd selected a print, she wheeled around again and admired the entire store. She filmed it in her mind like a videographer, eyes sweeping up one wall, down another, across to the drapes which Rosalie parted as she returned with two spicy mugs of chai. The cardamom and anise dominated. Marla inhaled deeply and slowly shook her head. "We have a lot of artists at the beach in Delaware, where I live, and their work is good, but this really floors me." She reached out for the chai and gave herself up to the moment, absorbing the atmosphere and drinking the milky tea.

"Maybe you'll be here twenty-five years from now," the shopkeeper quipped.

"Probably not." She sank into the chair again and stroked her chin as she thought of lobbying to Vern for an extended stay on the island. It was enough that he was allowing her to pursue the search for her ash man, as he called him. Marla got up again and browsed through the shop, holding her mug and sipping from time to time. "Are all these done by artists of St. Croix?" She traced her finger over a ceramic gecko and longed to touch a beaded mocko jumbie, the long-legged dancers of the islands. She felt the seed necklaces hanging from a display tree, pausing at the bigger seeds like her mother at her prayer beads. The silver metal clay jewelry stopped her in her tracks. "I have to have this." Tiny artists' palettes were crafted from the art clay into earrings. Dots of color represented dabs of paint. "I'll wear them the first day back to school."

Marla spent the rest of the afternoon in the boutique with her new friend. Rosalie set up a time the next day for exploring Mon Bijou and Peter's Rest.

"Is that a nursing home or a spa, Peter's Rest?"

"No, that's a section of the island. We have some

colorful names here – Lower Slob, Judith's Fancy, and these two are just a few of them."

"I knew that, but Lower Slob?" Marla laughed. "And I thought Lower Slower Delaware was funny." She explained how people in her half of the state were thought to be very laidback compared to areas closer to New Jersey and Pennsylvania.

The more they talked, the more it became obvious that Rosalie was a fellow artist and soulmate. She was captivated by ash man or woman, a notion she suggested to Marla.

"You know, I've always thought they were a man's ashes. Maybe because Vern calls him Ashman and Ashguy." She looked out the window toward the sea. "On the other hand, I've always been intrigued because of my mother's ashes." Marla felt like her friend could listen without judging her. "If her ashes got lost, no one could ever trace them back to me, but these ashes have a calling card, if only I could read it."

"You have to show me the box tomorrow. Too bad DNA tests can't tell us anything. Unless of course you have some bone or teeth in your box of ashes."

The thought of opening the plastic bag and examining the contents chilled her. A shiver went through her body. "I don't think I can open the bag."

"I can." Rosalie was like her mother with the let-me-at-'em attitude.

Marla grimaced. "I'll have to think about that." She didn't think she could ever open the bag, but she tucked the thought into a recess of her brain. "I haven't been real good at talking about this, much less doing something so drastic as handling the ashes." She looked at her watch. "For now, I need to go and meet my husband at the dive pier."

As she arranged her purchases in her shopping bag, she felt relieved the backpack and box were back at the hotel. The burden of finding ashman or woman was now a shared quest, and this had lightened the load more than the act of leaving the ashes in the room. Surprisingly, she felt optimistic.

Her guilt was gone now that she had faced down Vern and found him to be on her side. They had enjoyed the best sex they'd had in a long time. They were beginning to talk to each other with no computer interference. She had a friend who didn't act like she was the devil personified and who could help her search. And she had spent the afternoon surrounded by beauty and creativity, all augmented by the most delicious chai she had ever tasted.

What else could she hope for?

Steel Drum Magic

A steel drum band played on the beach that night. The gentle ponging of the rubber-tipped mallets on the steel pans reminded Marla of Harry Belafonte. When they played "Island in the Sun," Vern pulled Marla to the dance floor and crooned the song into her ear. "Ah, Harry, there's that voice I love," she said in exaggerated admiration.

He tried to raise his eyebrows up and down but succeeded in wiggling his ears instead. He fluttered his eyelashes and said. "I'm a man of many talents." With that, he pulled her close to him. "Let's go to the room and I'll show you some more."

After their lovemaking, they sat on the terrace with a fresh rum and coke. Usually they slept afterward, but this time they both were refreshed by their passion. Vern asked about her progress that day. "I wasn't going to talk about it. I didn't want to set you off and ruin what's turned into our best vacation ever," she said.

"It has been good, hasn't it? Maybe I'm growing up after ten years of not paying enough attention to my gal. Plus, at this ripe old age of thirty-five, I may not have many years left to appreciate you." He flashed his ironic smile. She returned it to let him know she'd detected the sarcasm.

Marla reached across the table for his hand and fondled his wedding band. Her engagement diamond caught the fading moonlight and glistened briefly as she lifted her glass. The waving palm fronds rasped softly and the water lapped below them. The steel drummers were still thrumming the steady Calypso beat over at the bandstand.

"Well?" His eyes bore a question.

Marla told him about the afternoon, Rosalie, the print she bought for Darryl, the earrings, and the plans for the next day. "She speaks English and knows just everybody! She thinks we should start at Peter's Rest. She's going to ask about Clemma Joseph and find her daughter's name."

"Well, you just be careful. Are you sure she's safe?"

"I'm one hundred percent sure she's safe."

"You know what they'll say when you disappear, never to be seen again." Vern leaned back on two legs of the rattan chair and braced himself against the stucco wall. "Vern did it. I'll be the greedy husband, looking to cash in on a million dollar insurance policy, if only we had one... Nobody will

93

believe me that I was diving and last saw you on the Christiansted pier."

Marla laughed. "You're the one who should be careful, swimming around with sharks and barracuda. I don't know why you love that so much."

"Sharks, no problem, *mon*. There was a guy on the boat named Sharky. He says you have to go way out to the outer reef to find good sharks to wrestle." His eyes took on a faraway look. "I wish you'd at least snorkel with me and see all those bright beau gregories, angel fish, fire coral, and scads of other colorful sights."

"Snorkel with you?" Marla grimaced at the thought of sticking her face in the water and breathing through a tube. "You know what they'll say when I don't return," she mimicked. She emptied the bottle of rum into their glasses and dared Vern to see who could chug their drinks down first. "I'd rather swallow this whole glass in one gulp than come face to face with either an angel fish or a shark."

"You can do both. Tonight the rum, tomorrow the angel fish."

"Tonight the rum, tomorrow Peter's Rest for me, Cane Bay dive for you. Let's go to bed."

Mon Bijou

Marla drove Vern to the Dive Shop. He was doing a two-tank dive and would be gone all day. Rosalie had promised to pick her up after lunch when her assistant could take over the shop. Marla parked the car by the Lymin' Inn. She crossed over the short footbridge that spanned the watergut and peeped in the shop windows as she made her way to the Sicilian parking lot intersection. A dumpster dog lay right in the center of the sidewalk. Many Crucian dogs were called by that name because that's where they got their food, from garbage left beside the containers or inside overturned bins. He watched her approach and raised his head when she was a yard away. She thought of the hounds at the LEAP and gave him a wide berth, but the dusty, short-haired mongrel merely beat his tail once against the stones and put his head back down.

At the end of the arcade, a chocolate-skinned man stood, watching her come near. His long-sleeved khaki shirt was stained with sweat at the armpits, his khaki pants were baggy at the knees, and his thin frame leaned against an arch. His smile grew wider as she got closer. She wished Vern were there with her instead of diving. She cut across the smaller parking lot and made a beeline directly to the side entrance of the tourist information center, ignoring him as he called out to her, "You need a taxi?"

Ellen's tourist agency looked like Disney World compared to this tourist information center, Marla thought, as she stood in the doorway taking in the long glass counter covering one doorless wall. A mocko jumbie on a small block of wood was on one shelf, accompanied by a ceramic sugar mill and a small basket of Cruzan Rum samplers. The bottles were adorned with hand-woven straw hats. The other two shelves were empty. The top of the display counter held a black rotary telephone – did that thing really work? wondered Marla, and a few brochures like the ones Ellen had given them, anchored into place by a piece of brain coral. The two walls which had doors were bare and the remaining wall had a cork bulletin board with phone numbers. Marla wasn't surprised to see that most of them were for taxis. Papers that weren't held down at all four corners fluttered whenever a breeze wafted through. An old faded poster of a Hobie Cat event and a more recent one of last year's

Carnival were screwed through their plexi-glas frames onto the same wall.

The Crucian woman seated behind the counter was reading a newspaper and didn't seem to care whether Marla wanted advice or was just passing through. Marla cleared her throat to announce her presence but it didn't faze the woman. "Excuse me," she said.

The woman looked up at her. "Good morning." Her emphasis on the "Good Morning" was delivered like a teacher admonishing a student who'd said "Ain't" and she waited for the proper response from Marla. She pursed her lips and sucked air through her teeth as the unsuspecting Marla stood mutely. Finally she said, "Do you need some help?"

Duh, thought Marla, no, I just came in to get out of the sun. "I wanted some advice on what there is to see here in town." She pulled the legs of her shorts down, trying to make them stretch over her knees as the woman again sucked her teeth and frowned toward Marla's bare legs. Marla thought back of the many flowing skirts and sundresses in Rosalie's boutique. She needed to buy at least one.

As the reluctant agent pulled out brochures and pointed toward different locations close to the main intersection, Marla started to catch on to the cadence and pronunciation of words. She was growing to like the language and thought about twenty-five years of living here like Rosalie and becoming "bi-lingual" but flinched as a pang of homesickness engulfed her.

Rebekah, the agent, became more lively as she told Marla about the town and the island, in general, and sights she could see in and outside of Christiansted. She wished she had brought the backpack downtown but winced at the thought of Rebekah's abhorrence if she knew she was carrying ashes. When Rebekah told her about the cemeteries and their colorful history, Marla broached the subject of the ashes from a different angle. "Where is the crematorium here on St. Croix?"

Rebekah's head jerked back and her pupils constricted. "We don't have one here. Why would you want to know that?" She backed away a little from Marla, and Marla thought she might be heading for the side entrance, the abrupt change showing in her face.

"Just curious." She thought quickly to come up with an acceptable lie. "A good friend just died last week and asked that his ashes be scattered in different places, so I guess cremation is still on my mind."

"Sorry," she said with the second syllable heavily accented the way the man by the roach coach had said the word two days ago. "Most people here believe in a proper burial. Cremations take place on Puerto Rico and no church or funeral home will perform a service with ashes."

Marla decided to leave this subject to a discussion with Rosalie. She thanked Rebekah and began her walk through Christiansted. No cremations on St. Croix. This very well could lead to a dead end. She tightened her lips at the irony – a dead end.

She visited the Fort and Government House, snapping pictures everywhere, seeing photo ops at every turn. Her feet were beginning to swell from the heat and so much walking. She had to be careful on the irregular sidewalks. The cobblestones rose and fell, many of them originals from the 1700s.

By lunch time she was exhausted. She thought about eating at the roach coach but didn't want to run into Owin and Seymour. She was feeling good about herself and dreaded the looks they'd give her, the aversion they would show. She poked along to the car, creeping alongside parked cars in the main square, cautiously looking for the two tour guides.

She spotted them mingling among the tourists. She'd heard another cruise ship was in Frederiksted. She was almost to her little silver Versa when the sweat-stained man called again from his shaded spot in the arcade, "Miss, you need a taxi?" and she answered, "I have a car." She pointed at the rental. "OK, later," he replied and scanned the area for another rider.

The sun was high in the sky, and the heat had sapped her energy. Marla was fit, a comfortable size ten, but she was not as careful about her physical well-being as the jogging, weightlifting, health food addict, Vern. At school there was a group who walked each day instead of eating lunch. Marla was not part of that group. In fact, just as she did at school, Marla had been thinking about lunch for the past hour.

Again she had spent the time without the cumbersome backpack and its ghost. She took a quick shower, changed into a different pair of shorts and top, and stashed the T-shirted box into her backpack. She slung it over her shoulder and climbed back up the hill to the terrace restaurant.

She visited the hotel's boutique first. Before I eat, she thought. She needed to buy a skirt for her wanderings with Rosalie. After Rebekah had glowered at her bare legs, she began to notice that it was mostly tourists showing flesh anywhere north of the knees. Marla liked her legs, the one body part she thought was near perfect. Her lumpy ear lobes, straight hair, common hazel eyes – these were all targets of her self-proclaimed poor body image. But not her legs. She didn't have Betty Davis eyes but she had Vern morph a picture on the computer, transposing her upper body over Betty Grable's legs on their fifth anniversary. He compared hers to the pin-up queen of yesteryear and decided, "Babe, yours are hotter." She was sure from the way he sometimes looked her up and down that he still admired them.

Marla judged the blue wrinkle-look skirt would be acceptable to Clemma Joseph or her daughter since it fell well below her knees, so she changed into it and jammed her shorts into the knapsack. Her pack was showing signs of wear. Outside it was fraying and dirty. Inside, the little box was deteriorating from all the movement, the peeling varnish flaking off and sticking to the T-shirt. She hoped its contents wouldn't spill out but shared the Crucians' repulsion and dared not transfer them from the box and certainly not from the plastic bag they rested in. She wanted to present them to the owner just as they were.

As she studied the menu, she reflected on what Vern's lunch would be like on the dive boat. Would it be the same mystery meat Owin and Seymour had packed for their tour? She thought it would be more in line with what they would usually eat – bologna sandwiches, potato chips, or other old stand-bys. She wished he were here with her, that he would be helping her along with Rosalie. But she was happy that he was enjoying his dives.

The dive boats were always packed with "statesiders," a term used to describe mostly white people although she had learned that many of the dark-skinned residents originally came from the States, too. Vern was beginning to make friends with the divemaster and crew. They were invited to join them at Davey Jones's Locker, a locals' bar in Gallows Bay, that night for a few rounds. Marla wondered whether he had discussed her mission with them and what they thought of it. She'd find out later.

She ordered baked brie. That shouldn't be something I'll drop onto my new skirt, she thought. It came with mango salsa and glazed figs. While she didn't drop cheese onto her skirt, Marla did dribble a spot of the tangy salsa onto her lap. She bent over, pulled the soiled part toward her, and wiped it with her napkin. She took her pack and hastily rushed to the ladies' room and scrubbed it again before hurrying out to meet Rosalie at the reception area. She wondered if Rosalie would be late like the tour guides, but as she rounded the corner, still dabbing at the stained spot, she saw her new friend striding across the terrazzo terrace toward the reception desk.

"Good afternoon, Cherise," Rosalie called out and the receptionist returned the good afternoon welcome. Marla was learning that the islanders never immediately launched into a conversation without a good morning, good afternoon, or a good night. Rosalie came toward her, arms stretched out, ready to embrace her. She looked like a *fashionista*, modeling wares from her shop. Her burnt carmine and cream caftan flowed easily, picking up the breeze that swept her through the lobby. A necklace hugged her throat, its dark brown seeds matched in color by the simple slouch handbag hanging from her left shoulder. Marla felt like a frump with her wet, stained ruffle skirt, navy tank top, and worn Jansport backpack.

More than that, she felt like a foolish frump. She had just spent a lunchtime, alone, in an exotic place surrounded by couples who were enjoying their vacations together. She was wearing a skirt she didn't want to buy. And for what? To visit a person who may not exist or be the one she was looking for? The box began to weigh heavily on her shoulder as well as her mind. What in the world ever made her think she could do this? Would Barney the woodworker win his bet? He said he'd wager against her finding the owner of the ashes. She knew she was getting closer and hoped to prove Barney wrong. Should she scrap the plan and salvage the vacation? But the bonds between her and Vern were stronger now than they had been in years. He was her protector and confidant, if she would let him be.

She stepped back from Rosalie's inviting greeting, unaccustomed to hugs. This was not something she grew up with. But Rosalie's beckoning brown arms pulled her in and her leather wristband caught on a strap on Marla's backpack, its four rings of tiger eyes begging for a peek inside. "Oh, clumsy me." Rosalie turned the bracelet and told it, "You naughty thing."

Marla found herself comforted by Rosalie. The woman seemed to understand her shyness, her unease. This was something her mother never quite got. Her mother, outgoing and lively, showed no fear toward anything. She approached life with a "take charge" attitude and often looked at her daughter as an anomaly. When Marla didn't want to go on a trip to Italy, she simply shrugged her shoulders and arranged a babysitter for her thirteen-year-old daughter. When Marla didn't apply for a summer grant to paint in the Adirondacks, her mother refused to pay for the art camp. They never discussed Marla's strengths, aspirations, or feelings; it was as though her mother couldn't waste time on such petty matters. Theresa Collin's one mistake, and it was a monumental one, was marrying Fred Hampton. She spent her post-divorce years making up for that mistake, beginning with taking back her maiden name. No second marriage to right the first one. No, her mother would never allow herself to fall in love. She never loved again. And Marla felt that included her.

She and Rosalie rode toward Mon Bijou. "I couldn't find out the daughter's name," Rosalie explained, "so maybe we'd better start with Ms. Joseph."

Rosalie's Godhood was now in question. She had felt sure this new savior would have all the answers figured out for her and that they would have gone directly to the daughter, found the mother, and ended the quest. Marla turned her thoughts to her arm, resting on the door frame. "I think I should put sunscreen on; I'm already starting to burn." She dug into her backpack and pulled out the plastic bottle, a flake of varnish sticking to it. "Do you know her address? Hendrix said he didn't know where she was now." She wondered if this was the first step in a new futility. She massaged some of her doubts as she smoothed on the sunscreen.

"There are hundreds of Josephs on this island. In Mon Bijou, I don't know how many. But believe me, somebody will know where Clemma Joseph is." She looked toward Marla, who imagined that Rosalie could see the question on her face. "There probably aren't too many of them that live on this particular street, but we'll find her, don't you worry." Rosalie adjusted her rearview mirror after bouncing through a pothole.

"Does anybody ever maintain these roads? I'll kiss the macadam when I get back to Delaware." Marla wiped the errant sunscreen from the doorframe and blew an exasperated breath as she saw a glob that had squirted onto her skirt. "My dishtowels at home look better than this brand new skirt!" She wiped the spot and smeared the cream on her face and inside arm.

"It'll be hard to get that oil out. Do you have another skirt or sundress?" Rosalie sounded the horn and waved to a man passing by.

He held a child's hand and moved to the shoulder with him. "OK," he said as he smiled and nodded his head. In his other hand, he was carrying a heavy burlap bag, resting it on his back. The little boy waved and thrust his head down, but his upturned eyes looked shyly at the passing car as he leaned against the man's side, waiting for the Honda to pass them.

"That's John Dunstan, used to be my gardener. His son became a famous lawyer in Bobby-lon. That's what they call the States – Babylon." She watched the pair in the rear-view mirror. " His son bought him a villa near here and he only does his own yardwork now. Great home. Moved his daughter and her family in with him and his wife."

"Must be nice." Marla twisted in her seat and regarded the pair as they became smaller. "He doesn't look like a rich man, though." His pants were baggy and so were the child's. His shirt was too big, he needed a shave, and he looked like he was carrying groceries in that bag. "You'd think he'd dress better and drive to the supermarket."

They had passed a small corner store that advertised salt fish and fifty pound bags of rice on special. John Dunstan looked like he was carrying the rice home. "I'm curious about his 'OK.' I've noticed that many people here say that as a greeting."

"You took a lot in! You must have a camera built-in to your eyes and ears. You're right. That is a common expression, 'OK.' And if you stay here long enough, you'll see that the people here are quite happy in their own way." Her bracelet rattled against the steering wheel as she downshifted to a lower gear. "They don't need all the luxuries you have in America."

Marla didn't think Rosalie was being judgmental, just giving an overview of rural life. Still, she noticed the *you*. "It sounds like you've pretty much removed yourself from America. But isn't this the United States Virgin Islands?"

"In some ways, yes, but you've already seen some of the differences, I'm sure, in your few days here."

"Really." Marla held tight to the armrest as Rosalie made the left into Mon Bijou. A hand-lettered sign revealed that this was the turnoff. Yes: dogs everywhere, lots of black people, curious spicy foods, no crematoriums, trade winds that blew whenever it became too stifling, Americans who didn't speak American. Yes, Marla had noticed some of the differences.

"Back to the skirt issue; do you have another?" Rosalie leaned closer to the windshield, reading street signs.

"Actually I packed light. The last time Vern flew, they lost his luggage, so we each brought a carry-on." She didn't tell Rosalie that she had to nestle the box inside her one bag so Vern wouldn't find out.

"I can always bring you something from the shop."

This kindness resounded in Marla. She remembered the afternoon she graduated from high school and her shoe strap broke. "I told you not to buy those shoes," her mother had scolded. "Maybe I can wear your white ones," Marla had begged. But it was not to be. "Good lesson," her mother had told her. "Always have a back-up plan." She had to wear her black pumps, no disaster, but a disappointment, one of so many.

The Honda slowed to a crawl. Marla's eyes lit up as she saw a mailbox standing on a pole with the name C. Joseph. Her voice shook. "Could this be it?"

"We'll see. Get out here."

Marla got out and Rosalie steered as close to the chain link fence as she could get, bright purple bougainvillea brushing against the side of the car.

They stood at the gate and Rosalie called out, accenting the first syllable, "*In*side!" More quietly she added, "In case there are dogs."

Getting no response, she opened the gate. It squeaked loudly and resisted her push. Rosalie's muscled arms gave another shove and the gate admitted them. Marla scanned the street to see if anyone would think they were breaking in. Everything was quiet. The metal louvers were closed tightly on this house and most of the homes within their vision. Only two other cars were parked in front of homes, one up on cinder blocks. Marla wondered if anyone lived in this neighborhood. It reminded her of a ghost town in the Old West she had seen on TV. A chicken bobbled its head and crossed the single lane, where it pecked and scratched next to an aloe plant.

"This is a working class neighborhood. Probably everyone's at a job." The pink stucco on the Joseph's walls was faded and desperately needed a paint job, as did several houses on the street. Overgrown poinsettia bushes, hibiscus, and bougainvillea poked through chain link fences up and down the street. At the corner, a Norfolk pine towered over all. Marla thought of her lonesome little pine in her living room, how she watered it carefully and kept Mo away from it. Here, these pine trees grew to enormous heights with no care at all. Another ping of homesickness pulled at her.

John Dunstan doesn't live on this street, she thought, or he'd whack those bushes back. And maybe Clemma Joseph, neither...They explored the yard. Marla sidestepped a pile of wood scraps. She had heard how centipedes and cockroaches hid in these cool spots underneath anything left out. An old refrigerator box slumped by an avocado tree where it had probably blown some time ago. Rains had reduced it to pulp with only one intact side.

In the back of the house stood an empty dog house, a thick length of chain prompting an image in Marla's mind of a Doberman who might have lived there. An arc of dirt surrounding the miniature house traced the path where he kept vigil, where he protected Clemma Joseph with his snarls and growls. But where was Clemma Joseph, or didn't she even live here? Might it have been Charles, Caroline, or Cassie Joseph? She shook her head and looked at Rosalie for help.

Rosalie seemed to read her mind. She drew closer to Marla and stretched her arms out again. This time Marla allowed herself to be folded into the embrace. "Don't worry, we'll get to the bottom of this or my name's not Rosalie McGee."

Marla laughed in spite of herself. "A real live leprechaun! Right here in the Caribbean. 'Tis my lucky day." Their shared laughter eased the tension, the build-up of expectations, the disappointment. She surprised herself at how readily she allowed Rosalie to hug her and thoughts of her mother came cascading again. The time her first boyfriend jilted her and how her mother had laughed it off. "Get used to it." What she had wanted then was a hug and reassurance that she was okay. The time she got a "B" in a literature class, her mother's special interest. She had tried so hard, but couldn't meet that teacher's expectations just like she couldn't meet her mother's. What she had wanted was a hug. What she got was, "Oh well, you never really were very good at reading underlying messages." She wasn't sure just when she stopped wanting and needing hugs and reassurances. But she remembered how she relished Vern's attentions, how his touch and soothing voice had opened up a new world to her.

"Let's walk around the neighborhood a bit." Rosalie led the way back out through the gate. The narrow road was deserted. About ten homes stood on each side of the street, and as they passed the third one, a dog startled them by throwing himself against a fence and showing ferocious teeth backed up by carnivorous snarls. Marla positioned her backpack on the side where the dog was. Rosalie noticed her move and said, "Won't do you much good, but not to worry. Let's just walk more in the middle of the street. It'll calm the hounds down a little."

Other dogs on the street responded to the canine alert system and came bounding from hidden places. Fortunately, all were within their own fenced yards. The chicken disappeared under a fence. Marla feared that a snarling dog could also get under such a fence. As a consequence of all the noise, a woman came out of her house at the end of the street. She was stout and had the gait of an arthritic, teetering from side to side. Her head was wrapped in a bright green turban, her dress and apron a clashing combination of fuchsia and Gulden's mustard yellow. She held a dishcloth and leaned against the fence with the cloth buffering the heat of the afternoon sun against the metal rail. The old woman, squinting into the intense rays, waited at her gate for the pair to reach her.

The minute she began to speak, Marla was relieved that Rosalie was there. The woman looked like a Carib Indian she had seen in a painting at the Whim Greathouse on the tour they had taken. She searched suspiciously for a hidden machete. In the past, the hostile Caribs had been very aggressive and reputedly had killed off the more peaceful Arawak Indians that had inhabited the island. This woman had the same high cheekbones and despite her gait, seemed very powerful with strong arms and piercing eyes.

Marla didn't understand one word, but Rosalie spoke to her in the same language. Marla had thought she was picking up the cadence and some of the strange words, but this exchange proved her wrong. She did understand *Ms. Joseph, Peter's Rest* and *Williams*. She also understood the last words the woman spoke. Rosalie thanked her, they smiled at each other, and the woman said, "God bless you and if you find Ms. Joseph, please tell her Anna sends her greetings." At this, the woman's face seemed almost angelic, and Marla was ashamed at the connection she had made to the warlike Caribs.

They returned to the car and Rosalie checked her

watch. "Do we have time to run over to Peter's Rest?" Marla was surprised it was so late. Even though the island was only twenty-eight miles long, it took longer to get anywhere with all the back roads and slow driving conditions. They'd barely have time to get back for her to pick Vern up at the Dive Shop. Rosalie offered to take them both back to the Buccaneer.

Marla exaggerated and told Rosalie she could drive from Fenwick Island to Philly faster than from Christiansted to Mon Bijou.

From the sparkle in her eyes, Marla could tell that Rosalie didn't believe a word of it. "It's a different world here," Rosalie said.

"Really." Marla could think of no better answer than the one she'd given earlier. "So what did that woman tell you?"

"Well, Clemma Joseph did live there."

Marla winced, disappointment showing in her eyes. She could see her painful expression reflected in the sideview mirror.

Rosalie went on, "But she left after her son disappeared."

"What's that all about?" Marla bounced forward, straining against the seat belt. "Could those be *his* ashes?"

"The lady said the daughter might know where she is now, but that they had had some problems. She didn't go into them." Rosalie stopped to let a school bus unload. The students ambled out, all in uniforms of the area high school, khaki pants and white shirts for the boys, burgundy pants or jumpers and white blouses for the girls. "The daughter's name is Eulalie Williams. We'll find her tomorrow, if we're in luck."

Traffic coming into Christiansted was crawling. Vern's group was expected back at four and it was now half past four. They came to a halt outside the towering Anglican church, a neo-Gothic landmark from the mid-1800s. Since traffic was stalled, Marla hopped out and took a quick picture. She marked on her mental calendar to visit St. John's before leaving. The harbor lay in the distance, what looked to be a five-minute walk. The bright catamarans and sunfish sails that had captivated them their first day stood out against the cerulean sea and ever-present puffy clouds. The Hotel on the Cay sat on its white sandy perch, its beach shaded by palm trees. She could see the tiny ferry boat making its way to the hotel. "How about if I get out here and meet you down in the parking lot by Lymin' Inn?"

Traffic was still at a standstill when Marla began

her descent down the main street. A mangy looking dog hung his head and looked toward her, and Marla crossed the street at the first intersection. Farther along a sweat-stained young man sat in an abandoned doorway, openly pulling from a pint rum bottle. Between swigs he rambled and threw his arms, gesticulating about some unknown disapproval, his anger seeming to grow with each swallow. Marla crossed back to the other side. Here's a different side to Paradise, she thought. She was outpacing Rosalie until she came to a level section of King Street. A car horn interrupted her trek, and she was happy to see Rosalie stopped, holding the rest of traffic back to allow Marla into the car.

"I can't believe they're not all blasting their horns," Marla said, pointing her thumb at the line behind Rosalie's Honda. " I've come a pretty good distance and you've all been creeping along."

"No problem, *mon*. Time, we have plenty of here."

"Maybe you do, but I don't. I can't believe it's already Tuesday and we're leaving Saturday. I have only one dive left."

"What's that mean?" Rosalie turned left toward the smaller parking lot and found a spot facing the water. She pulled up to the restraining log and looked at Marla. "One dive? You're going diving?"

"Hell no! I bought a five dive package for Vern and he's used up four."

"Well, can't you take him with you to finish this up? Surely he wants to see a happy face when the ashes are returned."

When the ashes are returned. Could that possibly happen? She replayed the impossible journey she'd made from the Fenwick Island beach to this exotic island, the keys that had opened massive barriers to get to this point. She stepped out of the car and saw that the boat was docked in front of the dive shop. Vern would be waiting impatiently for her. "It's a long story. I'll give you the details tomorrow. Come on with me while I get my knight in shining armor."

Marla expected Vern to be wearing a frown of disapproval because she was late, but when she and Rosalie stepped into the shop, he had a new glow. "So you're Rosalie, I presume."

He rose from the stool next to the counter and came toward them. For a second, she thought he might hug Rosalie. He seemed to be smitten by her. What was her secret ingredient? She felt a twinge of jealousy in the reception he was giving this stranger, but Rosalie took it in stride and treated Vern as though she had known him for years. "Vern, I'm glad to meet you. I've heard so much from Marla about you. Bob, from what I hear, you might have a new diver for your crew." Marla and Vern both looked toward the owner of the shop.

Bob came out from behind the counter and hugged her. "Where have you been, beautiful? It's been a long time since I've seen you on this end of the island." He held his arms out and admired her. "Still the fashion plate, I see."

A tourist pair entered the shop looking for information on dives and Bob left the three to take care of business. While he was explaining the different dive packages and showing them colorful brochures, Vern grabbed his wetsuit and motioned toward the door. He tilted his head when he caught Bob's eyes. "Later."

Bob acknowledged the message but broke away from the customers and called out to the retreating trio, "Bring Rosalie with you tonight!"

Davey Jones's Locker

They arrived at Davey Jones's Locker after nine. A treasure chest with glass beads and fake gold doubloons stood on a pedestal at the entrance. Inside it was dark, and Marla squinted, trying to find Bob in the dimness. Pirate flags hung about the bar and the cigarette smoke choked them. "Haven't they heard that smoke kills?" She was aghast that tables were crowded with patrons casually bellowing puffs of noxious fumes into the crowded room. She pointed to a poster that read: I'd love to drop anchor in your lagoon. The leering cartoon character bore the inked-in name Bill Travis, crossed out to read Norm Tunnel. "Either of those guys a new friend of yours?" she asked.

Vern laughed at the question. "Bob didn't warn me about this." He waved at the smoke cloud in front of his face. "I guess word hasn't reached here about no smoking. There he is over in the corner. I see he's saved us some seats." They wormed their way through the smoky watering hole, pulled the wooden captain's chairs out, and settled into them.

"Where's Rosalie?" were Bob's first words.

Obviously he wasn't a Crucian. No Good night, how are you? How's the family?

Marla mused over the fact that Rosalie had such an effect on everyone and explained her absence to Bob, that she'd had a long day and was going to go with Marla again tomorrow. Vern jokingly asked Bob, "You have a thing for Rosalie?" The other men at the table nodded in agreement to Bob's response that everyone who met Rosalie had a "thing" for her.

She was just one of those rare beings, Marla silently agreed. She had grown fond of the woman in the short time she'd known her. Rosalie was closer to her mother's age than hers and Vern's, but she had that ageless quality and that instant connectivity that attracted her like valence electrons or some remote term that she remembered from high school physics. Whatever it was, Rosalie had it. "What is it she's helping you with?" Bob leaned toward Marla as the noise in the club grew louder when the bartender increased the volume of the reggae music.

Vern frowned, which told Marla that he hadn't told them. But she ignored him. "I'm trying to find the owner of some ashes that washed up on the beach in Delaware."

"You've come all the way to St. Croix for that?

"Well, yeah, it seemed like a good starting point."

"From Delaware to St. Croix? Why not the Coast Guard? Capsized boats in the area?" Bob was clearly perplexed.

"Never thought of that," admitted Marla. She looked toward Vern who was following the conversation.

"But still, why St. Croix? What led you here?"

She told him about the mahogany, Barney the woodworker, and the words on the box.

"That's a long way off, though... But it's awesome. What are the chances that such a thing could happen. That you could trace this box from Delaware to St. Croix. Unbelievable!" Vern leaned in, seeming to get caught up with the search, too. "Still, what made you come so far? After you found out all those details?" Bob chugged a mouthful of beer.

"I'm still trying to figure out the pull this has on me. Rosalie has been such a big help." Marla told Bob of the reaction at the LEAP and how Rosalie was acting as her guide to Clemma Joseph. "I was almost ready to give it up after the LEAP."

"Well, you have to understand about Hendrix. His parents are from Haiti; a lot of that voodoo stuff's in his background." Bob took a swig of Corona and plunked the bottle noisily onto the wooden table, dislodging the wedge of lime and splashing beer in his face. She shook at the sudden action and he laughed. "That's how seeing the ashes probably affected him."

"I think we should take the box out on the next dive and give it a proper burial," Vern said. "And after that we can enjoy what's left of our vacation."

Marla's face fell, and Bob came back with a new suggestion. "We'll do that after she finds the owner and we'll bring her along, too."

The rest of the evening was filled with dive stories, tourist antics, and the various friends' accounts of their life on the island. Locals came to the table and pulled up more chairs until there was no room left. The highlight of the evening was the arrival of Sharky. "Well, shiver me timbers," he announced as he pulled up a chair and straddled it, his chest against its back. He held up his rum and coke and toasted Marla. "Me buxom beauty! What brings you here to this scurvy dive?" He waved his drink at the smoke cloud, the dim bulkhead lights positioned around the interior, the crowded bar.

Marla was delighted at the attention. His scraggly salt and pepper beard, the bandana blanketing his head, and the three missing fingers on his right hand enhanced his image. She spotted the tattoo of a shark with jaws wide open and knew immediately this was the legendary man Vern had talked about. His shark wrestling stories dominated the conversation until Marla's fear emerged. "Do you see sharks when you dive?" She glanced at Vern.

Sharky answered, "Don't worry, m'lady. He don't got enough flesh on them bones. They won't want him."

Everyone laughed and Vern ordered another round of drinks. Eric, one of the newest arrivals, told the newcomers that everyone at the table was a transplant from mostly cold weather states. "You should stay here a while. Marla, you could teach at the high school and Vern you can work with us a while, right Bob? Until you can find something else. Gannet Hardware is opening here soon; they'll need an office manager."

Marla and Vern looked at each other and each could read the other's knowing glance. No way, was what they both were thinking, but Vern said, "We'll think it over."

On the way back to the hotel, Marla asked, "Since you're not diving tomorrow, want to go with me to Peter's Rest with Rosalie?" She was surprised when he agreed. She looked out the window at the nightlife scene of Christiansted and saw her reflection in the glass. It smiled back at her. Maybe these ashes have a little of Hendrix's Haitian voodoo effect, she thought. How farfetched is that? Vern, agreeing to go? She wondered if *That Old Black Magic* had Vern in its spell, and the music from the 40's tune played in her mind as they returned to the Buccaneer.

Theresa Collins

That night Marla had a dream that her mother was there in the room with them. Her presence was so real Marla could smell her Miro cologne, an essence which Theresa had discovered in Madrid, then ordered online for years. She had splashed it on like aftershave on her neck, legs, belly, practically bathed in it. When she was too sick to drench herself with the fragrance, Marla wiped a cloth over her body with it.

In her dream, Marla smelled the Miro first; then the transparent Theresa Collins materialized. She was in her healthy body, not the wasted skeleton Marla remembered from her final days. She reached out to her, her arms those of Rosalie, tanned and muscular, and pulled her into her warm bosom. "My baby, how I loved you but could never show it."

Marla sat up in the bed and cried out, "Mommy." The transparent figure shimmered and disappeared.

Vern turned over. He jerked the sheet off and sat up, reached over to his trembling wife. "Marla, what's the matter?" He held her tightly and stroked her, petted her hair, kissed her cheek. "What's the matter?"

"Did you see her?"

"See who?"

"My mother."

Vern's sudden look of concern told her he thought she was hallucinating or had drunk too many Coronas. He settled on the logical explanation. "It was a dream, babe. Relax. It'll be OK."

Marla lay back down and turned on her side. Vern nestled her into his body and comforted her. She looked over to the backpack and saw that the moonlight had settled on the lump and that it seemed to glow from within, the outline muted by the T-shirt.

We

hey sat down to breakfast and ordered the daily special: coconut-banana French toast. After finishing his first cup of coffee, Vern was coming to life. "What time is Rosalie coming?"

"She'll be here at nine. Her assistant gave her the day off." She chuckled at the thought of having to get permission from an assistant.

"You're lucky she's taking the time to chase this down for you."

Marla wished he had said for *us*, but it was a rewarding turn of events that he would accompany her on the next segment of this journey, so she chewed thoughtfully and warped back to her nocturnal experience.

"Penny for your thoughts," Vern said, "and remember, no more secrets." He pointed his fork at the invisible bubble that was starting to surround her.

"I don't think it was a dream last night. I think my mother was actually there."

Vern bent his head and focused on whisking the bread around in the heavy syrup.

"Don't worry, I'm not wigging out and it wasn't a

hallucination unless someone slipped something into my beer last night." There was a decided calmness about Marla. "I felt her, Vern. Have you never heard of such phenomena?"

"Nobody I know has ever told me anything like that. I guess just because I didn't see or feel anything doesn't mean it didn't happen."

"So much has happened on this trip. You know what?"

"What?" He placed a penny on the table.

She laughed and snatched it, put it in her backpack. "I'm beginning to see the full reason I've been so obsessed. And I know how tolerant you've been through all this, so thank you."

He drank a mouthful of coffee and stayed quiet.

"Remember on the patio I told you I was still grieving over my mother?"

He nodded.

"Well, somehow I think these ashes touched me so deeply --- the fact that someone had lost them --- because of my mother. I think returning them made me think somehow that this was going to make up for the unresolved problems in my life." Her eyes teared. "That it would redeem me. Do you think that's crazy?"

Vern looked out to the sea, to the brightness of

the day. "Well, first of all, I don't think you need to redeem yourself for anything." His eyes bored into her. "But if anybody has ever worked hard for redemption, it's you. Crazy?" He tilted his head and with a wry smile said, "Only that you're so troubled by this." He reached out and took her hand. "We're going to find Ashguy and put this to rest, hopefully today."

We. The magic word.

Eulalie Williams

The trio began the trip to Peter's Rest. As she had promised, Rosalie had brought a sundress from her shop. The three piled into the little Honda and headed toward Eulalie Williams's home. Vern was sitting in the front seat with Rosalie. "How can you ever find anything around here?" he asked.

"I have good directions." She laughed. "We'll see a fish truck under a flamboyant tree and then at the next corner, we turn right." She shrugged. "At the second dumpster, we make another right. After that it gets a little tricky."

"Where did you get the directions? Did Miss Anna tell you that yesterday?" Marla leaned over the seat behind Vern.

"Actually Eulalie Williams is pretty well-known here. She's a supervisor at the Education Department. I talked to a teacher friend last night who'd been invited to a party at her home last year." Rosalie turned to glance at Marla. "Quite a spread she has. You'll get to see how the rich and famous live."

"Like John Dunstan?"

"I feel like a fifth wheel here." Vern looked back at Marla, then at Rosalie with a question on his face.

They replayed the events of yesterday and caught him up to speed. "Are you as excited about this as Marla is?" Rosalie asked after letting the events settle into Vern's mind. They drove around a taxi van parked in the middle of the street, the driver casually chatting to a passerby on the shoulder.

"Getting there. Never thought I'd say that." He twisted in his seat to catch Marla's eye. "But she's talked me into it."

His look pushed Marla's buttons. She beamed at the comment and smiled at Rosalie through the rear view mirror.

"There's our marker." Rosalie pointed to a spectacular flame red tree, so brilliant it looked painted. As expected, a truck with a cardboard sign waited under it along with two men on folding chairs, using a cooler as a domino table. They could hear the tiles clack as they neared the tree. "Want to buy some conch on the way back?" Rosalie motioned toward the sign that advertised the fresh caught conch.

"It's only 10:30." Vern eyed the men suspiciously. " How'd they catch it and get it here already?"

"You can be sure it's fresh. If you'd see how many people line up to buy there, you'd know it." Rosalie turned off the main road and the car bumped and jounced along the dirt road until it came to the second dumpster. The tall bush grass provided a wall, broken occasionally by dirt tracks leading to other settled areas. A bony hound walked haltingly in front of them, then stopped as if posing for a picture. "If you weren't here, I might pick him up," Rosalie said. "I already have three dumpster dogs." She laughed, slowing down as she drove carefully around it.

Turning in her seat to watch the dog, Marla remembered when she was eight years old, the time she brought a tiny kitten home. She had cuddled it and held it close while it purred and nursed her ear. She could hardly wait to show it to her mother. "You'll have to take that back where you found it," were her mother's first words. Marla pleaded tearfully and promised to feed it, clean the litter box, and vacuum any cathairs, but her mother would tolerate no chance of any attachment to an animal in her house. Now, Marla continued to watch the dog, still standing in the same spot, until it became a brown speck against the brown road.

She wanted to reach between the bucket seats and hug Rosalie. She wished Rosalie and her mother had met.

Her mother's appearance last night came back to her, and she recalled the happiness she showed when Marla finished her degree at University of Delaware, how proud she had been. Marla knew how pleased her mother was, but even then she was unable to embrace Marla, to verbally praise her. She overheard her mother telling friends how talented and sweet her daughter was, and her mother's students often told Marla of the rave reviews Theresa delivered in class. They followed Marla's progress, unknown to her.

They made the turn at the second dumpster. "Keep your eyes peeled." Rosalie explained that the estate was marked by two pillars. "They'll suddenly appear on the right somewhere in the next two miles." Her apologetic face directed itself again to the dirt road. "Not a very scenic road. But I love the aroma of the island, even on these dirty roads." She inhaled deeply. "When you're here a while you know where the frangipani trees are back behind the bush and where you can stop and pull up some marjoram or reach for some kenip along a side path."

They joined the inhalation and looked at each other. Marla said, "All I smell is thick, sweet, and dusty. Have to admit I don't know what any of these smells are."

Vern agreed.

"I can guarantee there's a tamarind tree right behind this stand of bush." Rosalie pointed to a section on the right side of the road. "There, see it?"

Marla spotted the tree, high above the tall grasses. "Those things look like dog turds hanging from the branches. What are they?"

Rosalie laughed. "Everyone says that, but they have the tastiest seeds inside. They make a paste of it. Kind of like gooey Sweet-Tarts. You often see kids walking around with paper cups, dipping their fingers into it."

They passed more ruts, side turn-offs, and a break in the tall grass. In the distance was a stand of cane. Rosalie explained that it was illegal to grow cane on St. Croix but in remote areas, people kept small parcels like this one.

"With all these dirt roads and twists and turns, I might make it to one of the Williamses' parties, but after a few drinks, I don't think I'd ever find my way out." Vern joked. "And this is an estate we're visiting?"

"Estate Madeline's Fancy, to be exact." Rosalie carefully avoided the deepest ruts, driving into the bush at one point, tilting the car. Marla slid across the back seat and Vern gripped the armrest. "Sorry, guys. This is a typical island road. You get used to it."

"Are those the pillars?" Marla spotted them as she was rearranging herself. Two tall coral and stone pillars stood out from the tan-tan plants whose weedlike growth dominated the roadside. Clusters of flat green pods framed the mahogany sign that identified Eulalie Williams' residence. *Estate Madeline's Fancy* was carved with the same swirling *y*, the curved *M*, the rhythmic expression of Edrick's hand. Marla would be able to identify his work anywhere. She reached over to Vern and touched his shoulder. "I think we've found the end of the story." She rubbed her diamond ring, her nervous excitement rising, and twisted it as they turned onto the entrance lane to the Williams residence. "I hope Clemma Joseph is here."

They continued up the long gravel road. While there were no ruts, they had to pause for several chickens and two goats who crossed in front of them without a sideward glace. Vern shifted in his seat, his knees nudging the door and leaned out the open window. "This is better than a night at the movies." A makeshift barn appeared to the right, its weatherbeaten slats revealing a vacant interior. "Is this a farm?"

"It probably was in the past. But I don't imagine our Ms. Williams is the farmer type." Rosalie studied the surroundings. On each side of the gravel road were open fields. Far back on one side was an ancient wooden windpump, missing most of its blades. Scattered fruit trees, groupings of decorative plants, and copses of grass stood in the fields. "There are horse farms, milk farms, and beef farms on the island, but if that were the case, you'd see lots of animals in the pastures here."

The Williams home sprang up before them. An old plantation house with a sweeping staircase leading to the second storey entrance welcomed visitors. The two storeys were covered with white stucco, green hurricane shutters on each window. The air plants growing in cracks in the steps and on the sides where plaster had cracked betrayed its age. They could see stone and coral beneath the flaking stucco. Rosalie parked next to a calabash tree, where a red Jeep was parked. "Be careful when you get out," she warned, pointing to the round green fruit hanging low. "One time, one of those fell on my head!"

Marla imagined how the lot looked the night of the party. There was space enough for at least ten cars, and her mind's eye saw the circular driveway and gravel path leading to the house, bumper to bumper.

"Let's find the entrance. I don't know if the main door is at the top of the steps or in the area under the pillars." Rosalie led them to the lower door. From inside came loud barks. Marla remembered the snapping teeth and bristled backs of other dogs she had seen in Mon Bijou and the LEAP.

Would they be welcomed here? She leaned into Vern as they waited for someone to answer the door. She was relieved that he was with her. His presence was a comfort, unlike at the LEAP, where she had still been harboring her secret. She recalled how hurt he had been and how that had hurt her, too. But he had ultimately comforted her there, even when her deceit was revealed. She was supported when he had come to her side as Hendrix reacted so angrily to the box of ashes. And now, again, he was her protector and partner. Now she could face any challenge. Leaning into him, she felt a glow of warmth like the early days of their love.

"OK, OK, calm down," came a voice from inside.

The door opened a crack and a woman looked out at them. She was an attractive dark-skinned woman, standing straight, her chin tilted upward, an inner strength emanating from her.

"Ms. Williams?" Rosalie asked.

She inspected them from head to toe and seemed to be deciding whether or not to continue a conversation. "Who are you?" she said.

"I'm Rosalie McGee from Frederiksted and these are the Alexanders from Delaware." Rosalie spread her arms, presenting the two. "Marla and Vern. They're looking for your mother."

"My mother? Why do you want her?" Her brow furrowed and she looked back and forth at Marla and Vern, then again at Rosalie. She slipped between the door and its frame, holding the dogs back with one leg. "Go back, Digger," she commanded the lead dog.

Marla felt safe from the dogs and pushed the box toward the woman. Her worst fears were surfacing. Perhaps this woman would react like Hendrix. Her hands shook slightly and her voice quavered. "I think this box belongs to her."

Eulalie's mouth fell open. Her eyes accused Marla. "Where did you get that?" She reached for the box and Marla instinctively drew it back, clutching it to her chest as she had at the LEAP.

"Is this your mother's? Is she here?" Marla demanded. Then she realized how rude she sounded and apologized. "I'm sorry. It's just that I've waited for this day to come and I'd hoped to find your mother. I want this box to belong to her." She offered the box to Ms. Williams and bowed slightly.

Ms. Williams gently took the box in her hands, her amber eyes filling with tears. She said to the group, "Maybe we'd better all come inside."

Eulalie led them into the living room. The dogs' nails clicked on the flagstones as they leapt and raced around them, tails wagging, begging for attention. "They sounded so ferocious," Vern said as he reached down and rubbed the smallest one's oversized ears.

"This is a beautiful home," Marla said as she took in the wicker furniture, teak tables, Tiffany lamps and wall hangings. She lingered at a small, brightly colored painting of Crucian homes. Rosalie joined her and together they looked at the miniature painting, a sugar mill in the background, trees clustered between the buildings.

Eulalie joined them and said to Rosalie, "I recognized you when you said you were from

Frederiksted." She nodded at Rosalie and gestured to the artwork. "I bought that Kit Cawley from your shop." She stood with them next to the painting of the houses, Cawley's signature white dots defining the edges of the roofs and the jet black background, another of the painter's trademarks.

"I remember that painting, but I don't remember seeing you in my shop." Marla watched as Rosalie looked at her again with new eyes, trying to remember her. Eulalie's elegant bearing and appearance, especially the luminous, light eyes against the dark skin, would have made an impression on anyone.

"You were pretty busy that day. Your saleswoman took care of me, a small, young lady, very pleasant, as I recall. Now let's sit down and get to the box and my mother." Eulalie's amber eyes were like a mood ring, and Marla saw the pupils constrict as she led them to a seating arrangement that faced the terrace. "Can I get you something to drink first?"

Marla detected an edge of nervousness in Eulalie's voice. "Maybe later," she said, hoping she would still be civil to her later. Her memory of Hendrix was never far away when it came to the chest of ashes, and now she hoped that Eulalie would not have the same response. She took a deep breath and looked from the box to Eulalie as she recounted her search from Delaware to St. Croix. Occasionally she turned to Vern or Rosalie and was comforted as they nodded their heads. When she got to the part about the LEAP, Vern reached over and took her hand.

"I can't believe it washed up in Delaware." Eulalie gripped the box more tightly and scrutinized Marla. "I'm amazed that you'd want to track this down."

"I hold my own mother's ashes dear." Marla nodded toward the box. "That exquisite box was proof that someone had the same attachment to those ashes."

Eulalie continued to stroke the box, its words, the smoothness of its finish. She seemed surprised by the barnacles and picked at them. "This was the last thing Edrick made for my mother before he disappeared. She used it as a jewelry box." She held it away from her body and placed it on the teak table, her eyes never leaving it. "Until she put his ashes in it."

Three heads jerked simultaneously. "Those are Edrick's ashes?" Marla was stunned. "What was her connection to him?"

"Edrick was her son, my brother."

Marla turned to Vern. "I wonder why Hendrix didn't tell us that."

"I think Bob hit that nail on the head. He couldn't believe you had those ashes and just freaked out."

"Where is your mother now?" Rosalie asked.

"The Herbert Grigg home." Eulalie looked down toward her lap.

Marla looked toward Rosalie and asked, "What's that?"

"A nursing home," replied Rosalie. "Named after a man who worked for the Health Department."

Eulalie nodded. "The hurricane last year disoriented my mother to a point that we had never seen." Eulalie looked out to the terrace, the red and yellow hibiscus plants in full bloom, the coleus plants' green and red leaves competing for recognition. Her eyes began to tear as she took in her garden. "She came here to live after that. She wandered through that garden day after day, looking for her box of ashes. She still asks for them."

Marla felt her throat tighten. Her own mother had never lost her mental faculties, but she grieved along with Eulalie at the loss of her mother, as profound as Marla's, perhaps even more so. "Do you think you could take them to her?" Marla pushed her hair back and hunched her shoulders as she leaned forward. She was on the verge of tears. "He must have been so special."

"Special he was. My brother Mervyn and I used to say my mother had one child only. How ironic that the ashes came to Delaware. We actually lived there for about three years. In fact, Mervyn still lives there."

Marla sat upright. Her mouth opened but no words would come out. Finally she looked at Vern and said, "Barney, the woodworker." She told them about Barney's apprentice Mervyn, and how that was the link to St. Croix and one of the four words carved on the box.

"Maybe Edrick was trying to unite 'allawe'," Eulalie suggested. She smiled sadly.

"I think I could use that drink you offered earlier." Marla's mouth had gone dry and her head was spinning. She breathed deeply to calm herself.

Vern put his arm around her and pulled her close to him. "This borders on miraculous." He shook his head. "Babe, remind me never to doubt your intuition again." To Eulalie he said, "I know it's early in the day, but I could use a drink, too.

Maybe one with a little kick to it."

Eulalie stood and pressed her skirt with both hands. She looked down at the box and gave it a soft pat. "I never drink before dinner, but I'll join you. How about you, Rosalie?"

"Count me in."

Marla rose from her seat and walked toward the patio doors. "Do you mind if I wander through your garden while you're fixing the drinks?"

Rosalie offered to help, and Vern and Marla slid the doors open. She tried to imagine Clemma. She pictured a combination of slim and attractive Eulalie and the determined and aged Miss Anna of Mon Bijou, weeping, prodding the ground with a cane, lifting the fern leaves, throwing her hands up to God, lamenting the loss of her son and his ashes. She took Vern's hand and leaned into him. "I hope she has enough sense left to recognize the box. And I hope it comforts her."

"Well, you've certainly done your part." He hugged her and they walked silently through the small botanical garden.

They all settled around the teak table again with rum punches and plantain chips. "Do you mind if I ask what happened to Edrick?" Marla said. She hoped she would not alienate Eulalie with the delicate question but was eager to hear the details of the box's journey and the loving Clemma.

"It started about three years ago. Edrick was bothered by something. We were never quite sure what it was. He was so talented and, in Mama's eyes, so perfect." She sighed deeply and continued. "And he truly was a gentle soul and an expert carver. He made the sign at the entrance to my home."

Marla nodded. "I recognized his hand in that."

"Anyway, Edrick decided he needed to leave the island, and he made this box as a going away present. I know this is very personal and you're strangers, but I feel a connection to you." Eulalie looked at each with a penetrating stare, one that burned through Marla's eyes and into her heart. She bent her head and continued, "We think he was being hunted by someone, drug dealers or someone who had a terrible hatred for him, although he was not the kind to make enemies easily." She noticed the shocked look on Marla's face. "And as far as we know, he wasn't involved in any way with drugs, but maybe someone was pushing him to use or deal. It's a way of life here with many misguided souls. Whatever the reason, he felt he had to get away. He didn't tell us why he had to leave, but we

knew it was a matter of *having* to not *wanting* to."
She reached down and patted the terrier that had
padded over and laid his head on her lap. The dog's
sad eyes met hers and she smiled down at him.

Marla thought of Mo and how he sensed when
she needed comforting, how he would curl up with
her and purr against her chest. She lifted the box
from the table and seeing how hard it was for
Eulalie, she tried to steer the conversation in a
different direction. "Do the words have special
meaning for your mother?" Marla turned the box
and read the four sides aloud.

"Oh, yes." Eulalie reached for the box and
touched each word as she explained. Afternoon
shadows fell on the box and darkened the carved
parts. Tears began to trickle and her voice broke
repeatedly. "He started with the 'Sorry' to tell her
how sorry he was that he was leaving. He knew
she'd say 'My peace.' She always did when she was
frustrated or baffled." A gentle trade wind carried
the perfume of the gardenia bushes from Eulalie's
garden to the small group. "My mother loves that
fragrance." She smiled as she continued with
'Allawe.' "He told her we would all always be
together." Here she had to stop. She blew her nose
and held the box close, as though it gave her

strength to continue. "And he ended with 'Irie' – he told her that every day would be an Irie day if she just thought of the family as being together, that his spirit would always be with her."

"And then he went away?" This was the first time Rosalie had spoken.

"Three years ago was the last time we ever saw him."

"How did your mother get his ashes?" Marla asked. "Did he come back here?"

"My mother wouldn't take his leaving as the final word. She used to be a pretty sharp woman. She tracked him down like the CIA. Even with privacy laws and such, she had a source at the airport and discovered he'd flown to Philly, so she booked a flight there." She addressed Marla. "She was even more determined than you. She figured he went to Mervyn. And it was true."

"Where was Mervyn living then?" Marla asked.

"Wilmington, Delaware. My mother showed up at his door, unannounced. The really sad thing is that she led his trackers right to him." She hesitated. "She didn't know he was running away from them." Eulalie clasped her hands together in her lap and opened them as her terrier edged closer, shoving his nose into her hands.

"If you'd feel better, we'll just leave the ashes with you now and go away." Marla stood tentatively and reached out to Eulalie. "I know how hard this must be on you." She smiled at the little dog with his funny pointed ears and his healing powers. She petted his wiry head, but he didn't respond to her touch. "I'm sorry that we've caused so much sadness."

"No, please stay. You've come so far and probably have questions."

"This sounds like it's none of our business." Vern rose from his seat, too, and gently pressed Eulalie's hand. "It must be so very painful for you."

"Thank you, but you've made it your business by bringing the ashes here." Eulalie lifted her chin and said in a strong voice, "I have to admit I'm as curious as you probably are about how the ashes washed up in Delaware."

Marla nodded in agreement.

"My mother carried that box everywhere. After Edrick's murder... I really can't bring myself to talk about that." She breathed deeply, shuddered, and looked out to the terrace. "My mother couldn't come home without him. She'd gone to Delaware to bring him back, and she did, at least what would fit in that box he had made for her." At this, she took her hands from the dog and buried her face in them. She remained silent, but her shoulders trembled. After taking a few deep breaths, she continued. "Part of her died with him, and then more died when she lost the box."

"How did she lose the box?" Vern had returned to his seat but was leaning forward, hanging on every word. "Did someone steal it from her?" His voice carried a trace of anger.

Marla saw that Vern was in his protective mode and silently admired him. She knew he was a full partner now, that the quest to return the ashes was his, too.

"Remember, I mentioned a hurricane? When the last big one swept over the island, she happened to be in Christiansted. At church as a matter of fact, when the intense winds whipped up." She shook her head. "She thought she'd be safer there than trying to get here or back to Mon Bijou. Curiosity got the better part and she poked her head out to see what was happening. Before anyone could reach her, the wind carried her outside. She was holding the box and it blew away." Eulalie frowned at the threesome as if assessing whether or not they were believing this account. "She tried to chase after it, but two men pulled her back inside and were able to bolt the door."

Marla picked up the box and thought of her mother's ashes. She could only imagine the grief that struck Clemma. A mother losing a son twice. How tragic. "Why did she have the ashes with her?"

"She always had those ashes with her. They were in her handbag at the time. She never left the house without 'having my boy with me,' as she said."

"The box doesn't seem banged up. I wonder how it reached the water intact and came so far." Vern gently picked the box up from where Marla had returned it to the table. He held it up to the afternoon light and turned it, feeling its sides.

"Have you ever been in a hurricane?" Eulalie trembled- perhaps at the remembrance of the effects of previous storms. "It's not that far from St. John's church to the water. It probably never landed until it was past the reef. We never found her bag, of course. And she had had that box specially sealed by the funeral home in Delaware. So I guess that made it a very seaworthy little vessel."

Marla recalled stories Rosalie had told them of that hurricane: the twisting of steel rods, ripping off of roofs, defoliation of every tree on the island. She thought of the day she walked from the church to town and Rosalie picked her up. She could easily imagine the handbag soaring through the air that short distance and into the sea.

Eulalie stood up and straightened her dress. She removed the tray from the table. Then she let out a long breath and looked down at the three visitors. "I need to call my brother Mervyn and also let my husband know about this. We'll decide how to approach Mother with the ashes."

Marla twisted her ring and took a loving look at the box, savoring it, her face beaming in contentment. "I'm so happy it's turned out like this. I hope it lifts your mother's spirits."

"Maybe you'd like to see her before you leave? How much longer will you be on island?"

The Obeah Men

Marla and Vern went with Rosalie for dinner at Ohna's, a local restaurant. Rosalie told them if they really wanted the island flavor, that was the place to go. Not far from the Buccaneer, it was a continent away in appearance, with the tables and chairs more typical of a church basement. The simplicity of the restaurant was overshadowed by the magnificence of the cuisine. As they passed the various tables, the spices and seasonings of the dishes made Marla's mouth water. The thyme and green onions of the seasoned rice mingled with coconut milk, peanut sauce, and cumin in the tantalizing concoctions they saw. The clinking of cutlery and animated conversations set the stage for a most interesting culinary experience. They read the menu and Marla and Vern decided to try two West Indian specialties: bullfoot stew and kalaloo with fungee. Rosalie ordered a traditional chicken and seasoned rice dish that Ohna was known for.

"Today was certainly a surprise." Marla sipped a ginger beer and continued, "Anything would have been a surprise but ---Edrick? I really never would have imagined that."

"To me, Mervyn was the bigger surprise." Vern shook his head. "Actually this whole thing surprises me." He poked at his leafy green stew, and for a moment, Marla was uncertain whether this was the surprise he was talking about. A green leaf hung from his lower lip and Marla scooped it with her spoon and fed it to him. They all laughed.

Rosalie added that she was curious about Edrick's death. She was surprised that word hadn't exploded over the island. Edrick was a popular figure, a well-known and respected carver. "There's more to this story." She held her fork in the air and paused, her elbow on the table and stroked the fork back and forth like a metronome.

Ohna was making her rounds, as was her custom, Rosalie explained. "Good night, my friends," she said, stopping at their table. "Wha' wrong, Rosalie, your fork ain' workin' right?"

Rosalie laughed and said, "Ohna, my fork's always working here." She put it down and changed her tone. "But my mind is having a small problem. Maybe you can help me out."

"You know I'm always one to please, darlin'. What's the problem? First of all, who are your guests? I've never seen them here before." She smiled at Marla and Vern, showing a gold upper canine. The gold tooth was matched by a heavy rope necklace and assortment of thick gold bracelets, brilliant against her ebony skin.

After the introductions, Rosalie got to the point. "Ohna, do you know anything about Edrick Joseph?"

Ohna's eyes darted about the restaurant. She leaned toward the table and glanced at the two newcomers, then back at Rosalie. "What do you mean?" Her voice betrayed a tinge of fear.

Rosalie explained why Marla and Vern were there and that she was surprised she had never heard anything about Edrick's leaving and subsequent death. "I just find it a little strange that nobody has ever mentioned something about this."

"There usually isn't something like this. I only know it involves a little Obeah, and that isn't something I want to get mixed up with."

"So it wasn't drugs and drug dealers or moneylenders after him." Rosalie nodded in understanding. "I can't understand why his sister felt he had to leave the island. I've sold a few pieces done by Edrick..." She sipped her passion fruit juice. "He wasn't showy; he always seemed so clean-cut and wholesome. I wonder what really happened to him."

"If Ms. Williams isn't telling you, I don't think anyone will." Ohna wiped her hands on her floral apron and then rubbed them together, as though she was washing her hands of the issue.

"Except perhaps Clemma Joseph. If even she knows. Sun rose and set on that boy."

"But would she want them thinking Black Magic played a part?" Vern's face lit up as he said this. "That is, if it did."

Marla recognized the look as one he took on during the interactive video games he played at home. She watched Vern's face beam and she shivered. The sound of Black Magic and finding out what happened to Edrick were not part of her quest, and she wasn't sure she liked the direction they were turning now.

Ohna moved away from the table and surveyed the restaurant again with furtive eyes. She came back and bent over Rosalie, close to her ear. "I don't like the mention of Obeah or Black Magic here. That's powerful stuff." She tilted her head toward the pool table where the two players had located themselves closer to where the diners were, their heads inclined as though they were picking up strands of the conversation. "Before you leave, come back to my private quarters."

Ohna left the table and headed back to the kitchen. Patrons pushed their chairs away from tables and welcomed her to join them. A key to the popularity of the West Indian restaurant was this cheerful woman, Marla instinctively knew. Wooden tables with white paper tablecloths and metal chairs with bright red plastic seats, notwithstanding, this was clearly a beloved and popular spot. Marla watched as Ohna adjusted an arrangement of fresh-cut hibiscus at one table and leaned back to admire her work. The four at the table all raised thumbs up and she left them all smiling as she continued to the back.

As Ohna backtracked toward the kitchen, Marla turned her attention on the pool players. The dividing wall sporadically hid them as they moved around the table, trading shots. She heard the balls crack as one player broke the rack and the muted bouncing off the side rails as play continued, followed by more cracking, ball against ball. The decorative cement blocks in the dividing wall were incised in geometric patterns to allow air to circulate and to give the restaurant a bigger appearance. She noticed the younger one tracking Ohna's progress. The two came close together, whispered something to each other, and resumed following her progress.

They reminded her of thugs, the ones she used to think of when she thought of Hell's Angels. They both looked like they needed a good bath. The older one had greasy hair and a frayed T-shirt, slit into a V at the neck. The younger one turned toward Marla and stared directly at her. She stared back, pinned motionless by his piercing gaze. He slowly nodded his head and rested the cue stick against his hip while he chalked its tip. He bent his head, the New York Yankees cap shielding his eyes and he aligned his body to deliver the next stroke.

"He gives me the creeps." Marla shuddered.

Vern took her hand and massaged it. "Your hand is like ice. Who gives you the creeps?"

"The little guy with the Yankees cap and the cigarette hanging out of his mouth."

Rosalie looked through the dividing wall at the object of Marla's fear. She swallowed a bite of chicken and softly said, "I'm beginning to think you're a little psychic. That's Sammy Abramson. He's big trouble."

"What about the partner, the one with the tattoos everywhere?" Vern asked as he sized them up, and Marla was afraid he was considering taking the two of them. He lowered his eyebrows and pursed his lips. She had seen that look when he was a lifeguard. Once when a bather refused to come in when he whistled, he started out for him, afraid he couldn't swim back to shore. When it turned out the swimmer was "just playin' with ya," Marla had seen that look, his dead serious look. He watched the bather like that for about twenty minutes after the incident, the same as he was now watching the pool players.

"Double trouble," Rosalie said. Still speaking in the softest of voices, she continued, "They're why Ohna didn't want to continue the conversation. Some people say Sammy's an Obeahman. His buddy, Ophi, is his 'yes man,' does everything Sammy tells him." She finished eating her chicken and rice and watched the men watch them. "I think they have an interest in us."

Marla pushed some stew around in her bowl while Vern drank his beer, but neither took another bite of food.

The two came over to the table, still holding their cue sticks. Sammy's eyes smirked at Vern; his lower lip was turned down, a grin gone wrong. He addressed Rosalie. "Good night, Rosalie. I see you have guests. May we have the pleasure of meeting them?"

"We were just leaving," Vern said. He met Sammy's eyes and didn't waver. It was a smackdown, a cockfight, a meeting of strong wills. He got up from his seat, still staring and said to the women, "Let's go and say good-bye to Ohna." He looked directly at the other man's left arm, a serpent tattooed from above the elbow with its fangs and tongue reaching out as he opened and closed his fist. He shifted his eyes to the man's eyes and shot an unblinking stare at him as they left the table.

Marla could feel their eyes burning into her as she made her way through the restaurant to the kitchen. She was anxious to hear what Ohna wanted to tell them privately, but the searing feeling in her back warned her they needed to leave.

Ohna saw them coming as she stood on tiptoes and peeked through the circular windows separating her from the dining area. She ushered them back to her office and said, "Let's make this quick. I don't want any dealings with those two, especially over Edrick."

They exchanged worried glances and Marla looked toward the dining area to see if the men had followed them into the kitchen. Ohna said, "I don't know if those two know anything, but they were too interested in our conversation at the table. And - they have a bad history here on the island. They might get some strange ideas if you're in here too long, so I'm just going to walk out with you and act like we're old friends, like your guests lived here a while back." She added, "Meet me at Sunny Isle tomorrow, at noon. I'll be coming out of Woolworth's. We'll talk then."

As they returned to the kitchen, Marla saw the one called Sammy watching from a distance through the circular windows. Ohna introduced the three to her daughter, who was preparing a pot of West African vegetarian soup. Marla sniffed the brew and the daughter offered her a taste. The trio lingered at the various pots and tasted bits of culinary delights, although Marla had lost all enjoyment for food, constantly checking to see where the two men were.

Together the foursome left the kitchen, smiling and talking in normal voices, which seemed exaggerated to Marla, but she realized Ohna and Rosalie were putting on a show. She knew Vern was going along with them but that he never lost focus on the pool players. Ohna stood on the patio at the entrance to the restaurant and waved good-bye.

"Please come back again," she called in a loud voice as they drove past her in the parking lot. "And give Roland my love."

"Who's Roland," Marla asked Rosalie.

"You got me. I think she just threw the name in to give us familiarity."

As they left the parking lot, Marla caught Sammy watching them through the decorative cement blocks. He sneered at them and shivers ran up her spine.

A Feeding Frenzy

How about a little tennis this morning before it gets too hot," Marla said. "This is such a lovely hotel and we've spent practically no time here." From their breakfast table on the terrace, they could see the courts, down by their wing. A pair of early risers was already at it, and the ponging of the ball against the hard court inspired Marla.

"I was thinking it might be a good idea to drive over to the LEAP and have another go at Hendrix. My final dive is tonight and I want to meet Ohna with you and Rosalie, so maybe we could go there after breakfast." Vern spooned some sugar onto a saucer and set it at the edge of the table. Within seconds, a tiny yellow bananaquit perched there, looked at the two of them and began pecking at the treat. Vern laughed, silently. Marla loved this quiet way about him. Sometimes he would nudge her and point at Mo, stalking an ant or mosquito, not wanting to interrupt the cat and now not wanting to frighten the bird away. "Maybe Hendrix will talk to us. Maybe he knows more about this than he was letting on."

Marla was surprised. "I don't know. He seemed pretty spooked by us. Rosalie's working at the shop until she goes to Sunny Isle, and I'm not ready to take Hendrix on without her." Her instincts were to avoid Hendrix, not include him. "Besides, we've found the owner of the ashes. Why do we need him, or anyone else, for that matter?"

"Let's give it a try anyway. We'll play tennis tomorrow. On the way to the LEAP, you can show me Rosalie's shop."

Marla recognized Vern's determined look and acquiesced, although the whole idea of the angry little man upset her. She no longer wanted her waffles and fruit syrup, a meal she had relished nearly every morning. She watched the little bird peck away at the sugar and took in the beautiful colors of the bougainvillea, hibiscus, turquoise sea, white beach, and hills surrounding the complex. She decided this heaven had to have a little hell in it, too, and she could face Hendrix as long as Vern was with her.

They drove down Centerline Road. This was Vern's first real look at the island other than the tour with the guides. "Now I know what they were talking about when they went into the jungle and brought all those bodies back from Guyana." He put his hand over his mouth and nose every time they neared a dead, bloated animal on the side of the road. "Once you smell death, you always know it, I suppose."

"I wonder if we'll ever find out how Edrick died?" She immediately regretted saying this. She knew this was playing right into Vern's interest in the case, and she instinctively knew this could be trouble. Why don't I follow my instincts, she thought, and looked away from Vern and centered on the roadside activity, people walking on the dirt shoulder, trash dropped carelessly along the sides. In spite of the unkempt appearance, the natural beauty of the island trumped all. She looked beyond the roadsides and into the fields, the rolling hills, the elaborate homes tucked into niches high above the flat areas, the variety of trees. She inhaled the mixed aromas of sweet, musky, pungent. Again that "island smell" she loved.

"How about if I call Darryl and get him in on this? I guess Edrick was killed in Wilmington." Vern was animated. "Remember his cousin, Cliff? He's a State Trooper at the Wilmington Barracks. Maybe he can ask him if he knows anything." He gripped the steering wheel and nearly moved into the right lane.

"Watch it!" Marla reached for the wheel and righted the car. A startled driver shook his fist at them. "That was a close one."

"Guess I should have left the driving to you." He smiled sheepishly. "When do you think Edrick was killed?"

Marla had hoped the near accident would have driven his mind off the topic, but Vern seemed to be hot on the case. She recalled when they played Clue, how he would practically jump out of his chair when he was closing in on the killer. Edrick was no Colonel Mustard, nor was Vern the Ace Sleuth, but it was clear to Marla that there would be no turning back now for Vern. She could see the wheels turning in his head as he kept his eyes on the road, missing any opportunity to sightsee.

"Well, remember Hendrix said he left the island three years ago." Marla searched her memory for the details they'd gathered. "And Clemma tracked him down. Then there was the hurricane, so probably within the last two years."

Vern pulled into the long drive leading to the University and followed it to the parking lot.

"Why are we stopping here?" Marla asked.

"Number one, it's hard enough staying in the left lane," answered Vern. "Plus I'm hoping to get a good connection in the open space." He got out of the car and hit the speed dial to Darryl. Waiting for an answer, he admired the tall royal palms that lined the entrance and the lay-out of the campus. Low buildings with red tile roofs and yellow painted cement blocks nestled in the rolling landscape. "Working for Gannet Hardware might not be so bad," he mouthed to Marla as he pointed to the landscape.

Still sitting in the car, she grinned and thought back to the beginning of the entire trip, finding the box, the anxiety of whether or not to tell Vern. They had come so far. Leave it to Vern, she mused, to want to get to the very root of this case. He was a greater bloodhound than she was. Now he was the leader of the quest, and although she was happy to accompany him, it was a little unsettling that he had taken over her mission.

He settled back into the driver's seat and turned the ignition key. "Darryl's on it. He's going to call Cliff." Vern fastened his seat belt. "This is getting more and more interesting by the hour. Darryl even wants to get in on the big investigation."

Surprise, surprise, thought Marla. Darryl was always Vern's main competitor at Clue. Whenever the two played, one or the other solved the murder, no matter how many other players there were. But this is no game, Marla reminded herself.

She checked her watch and was relieved to see they would not have time to drive to the LEAP, see Rosalie's shop, and get back to Sunny Isle to meet Ohna. She suggested some random drives down side roads. They ended up at the sea on their first side trip. Vern parked on the dirt shoulder and they got out to explore. At the end of the road was a watergut, a cement path that led directly from the road into the water. Fishermen would launch their boats from here. When they returned they would clean the fish from this spot and throw the bloody parts into the water. Marla heard a snapping and thrashing sound. They walked to the depression in the beach and the noise got louder the closer they came. "Those are shark fins!" Vern pointed to the roiling water where the sound came from. "At least five of them."

Marla looked toward the sound. The fins and backs of the sharks' bodies surfaced and plunged through the pink, bloodied water. Snapping teeth, flat, black eyes, carcasses of huge fish horrified her. One shark launched himself practically onto the beach and was carried back out by the next wave. Marla gasped... "Do you really have to do that dive tonight?" She backed away from the feeding frenzy and pulled Vern with her. The smell of blood was making her sick. It stood out above the saltiness of the air, the heaviness of the roadside ferns, the sweet yellow allamanda in the nearby yard.

He rolled his eyes and allowed her to lead him away. "Marla, you've got to understand. They only come here because fishermen leave the bloody parts here. See those carcasses?"

"Remind me not to come here to sunbathe."

He walked her to the car. "You stay here. I want to go watch a few minutes. I've never seen anything like this." His eyes lit up, and she knew it would be cruel to keep him from it, so she agreed to let him watch.

"But don't get too close!" she called as he approached the site.

Vern stayed until the sharks were finished with the remains of the fish, then returned to the waiting Marla and with a satisfied smile, opened the door and slid behind the wheel. "OK, let's get over to Rosalie's." He looked over at Marla and said, "My God! Marla, you're green." She heard the surprise in his voice but also the amusement. "I thought that only happened in books." He stared at her in amazement.

"It's not funny," she said. "You know how scared I am of you diving. And that little scene sure didn't help." She bent forward and folded her arms around her waist, pressing on her stomach.

Sunny Isle Shopping Center

When they entered Rosalie's shop, she and her assistant had their hands full. A cruise ship was berthed in Frederiksted and tourists were in every corner, trying on hats, fingering the jewelry, holding batik wraps up against their bodies and checking for color compatibility in the various mirrors. "Can we help?" Marla whispered.

"Just see if any goods walk out on their own," Rosalie whispered.

Vern positioned himself at the door. A uniform on his tall, muscular frame would have warned off any would-be shoplifters. Marla noticed one woman giving him the once-over and kept her eyes on her. No chance she could steal him. Her twinge of jealousy amused her. Again she realized she had never loved him more than she did on this trip. She wondered if the surge of emotion would wane when they returned to their normal routine, when there was just the simple, beautiful but boring coast of

Delaware, the humdrum daily activity, the crowded highways, the mundaneness of it all.

She picked out a lime green sundress to add to her growing collection, held it against herself, and winked at Vern, who was watching her every move. His rapt attention brought on a wave of desire that shook her. He rubbed his fingers together and then made a flying away motion with his hand and lifted his shoulders in resignation. Marla knew he didn't mind spending the money, so she added a seed necklace to the purchase. She hoped his thoughts were as erotic as hers, that he was picturing her in the dress and thinking of disrobing her.

The burst of business ended abruptly as a horn sounded outside. It was the cruise ship's bus to Christiansted. The shoppers paid for their purchases and filed out and onto the bus, sunny yellow bags with bright red hibiscus blossoms and *Rosalie* written in flowing purple script. Beneath the name was her Frederiksted address. They would carry her advertisement across the island and back to the States.

Rosalie prepared chai while Marla directed Vern to the planter's chair. "We really have to get one of these," he crooned as he molded himself into its contours.

The four sat together and chatted; then Rosalie dismissed her assistant for the afternoon. "Turn the *Closed* sign around as you go out, Diarra. I don't think there will be another rush today."

"Is this good business? Are you losing money on us?" Vern sat up in the chair, pulling his legs off the extensions.

"There isn't enough money in the world to keep me from this now." Rosalie went to the cash register and removed the morning's take. "Eulalie Williams called me early this morning. She's taking the ashes to her mother this afternoon." Her eyes brightened as she remembered the conversation. "I asked her to do it later... so we wouldn't miss Ohna."

"She wants *us* to come?" Marla's hand sprang to her chest.

"Did you tell her we were seeing Ohna?" Vern asked.

"Yes, she wants us to come and no, I didn't tell her about Ohna. I don't know how much Eulalie really knows about Edrick's death. I thought I'd be quiet about that for now."

They all piled into Rosalie's Honda and turned back onto Centerline Road for the trip to Sunny Isle. They passed the University where Vern had made the phone call. Rosalie told them how the tall palms had been blown away by one forceful hurricane and how proud everyone was that the new ones had grown so quickly. Marla pictured Clemma's handbag blowing toward the sea, launching the ashes on their way to the Delaware shore.

As they continued along, they saw the students who were attending summer school taking a break outside the sprawling high school. Marla was surprised that all the public schools had designated uniforms. "Remnants of the British system, I suppose," Rosalie told them. The heat was increasing as the noon sun bore down on the island and the students searched for shady spots under the eaves and in the taxi bus stand at the side of the road.

A line had gathered at the roadside vendor by the school. His wares were stacked on rudely-constructed beams and planks, and the down-islander stood under a worn canopy, devised from a catamaran sail. Cars were parked on the shoulder and buyers waited patiently in the hot sun for purchases of fruit juice, mangoes, hands of finger bananas, and tamarind paste in the cups Rosalie had described.

Farther along the conch sellers were in place and Marla remembered the thrashing of the sharks. A sign advertised fresh red snapper and barracuda, in addition to the conch. She recognized the dilapidated black truck as the one they had passed earlier on the way to the feeding frenzy. "I always heard you shouldn't eat barracuda," Marla said.

Rosalie explained the practice on St. Croix. "Islanders have it down to a science. They always cook it with a potato. If the potato turns black, it's a sure sign to dump it."

They rounded a bend and a sweeping parking lot and shopping center came into view. "OK, here's Sunny Isle." It was much like any shopping center, anywhere. If it weren't for the brilliant flamboyant tree in the center, rows of purple, orange, and red bougainvillea in planters between the parking sections, and the "island smell," Marla thought it could have been the Rehoboth Mall. Marshall's, Woolworth's, Pizza Hut franchises occupied the space along with a cinema. Unfamiliar to her were the Grand Union Food Market, and Banco Popular bank plus a few local vendors. A woman selling VI lottery tickets sat at a card table and waved a handful of the colorful coupons, but a man gestured her off with a smile and motion of his hand, signaling a silent, No thanks.

Rosalie found a parking spot near Woolworth's and they began their surveillance. They had timed it so they would only have a few minutes to wait. Rosalie's car had no air conditioning, so they sat with the windows rolled down until Vern had had enough. "I'm going to take a little stroll," he said. All three left the car and made their way toward the line of stores nearest them. At exactly twelve o'clock, Ohna came out, carrying two bags of goods. They walked toward her and in mock surprise greeted her. The tiny woman hugged her bags close to her and called out as though she also was amazed at her good fortune to run into them. There was a bench near the Grand Union market, and the four headed toward it. She situated her bags at her feet and they began their talk.

Ohna told them what little she knew. There had been a cloud over Edrick's disappearance and assumed death. News had leaked out that Clemma had his ashes in the box she carried with her, but no one could verify it. "It was all hush-hush. Clemma Joseph was a changed woman when she came back from the States, but she would never talk about her trip there or her missing son." She scanned the parking lot. "Mervyn brought her back here, but he only stayed long enough to take her home and visit his sister. The family didn't even have a funeral, just a private memorial service. Everything was kept secret, probably because of the Obeah rumors. Mervyn caught the next plane back to the States."

Ohna's eyes reflected pain as she continued the story. "Every once in a while, Clemma would mutter when she was walking in town or at church, and I suppose the stories started that way. People overheard 'Obeah, murder, Edrick' from time to time and the news leaked out." Here she stopped and held her hands out. "But you know how powerful Obeah is here and no one would think of getting caught spreading the story." Her eyes swept the parking lot again. "Rosalie, I know you a long time, but I don't want to mention this again." She took her hands in hers. "I hope you can understand that."

"Of course, Ohna." Rosalie squeezed the little woman's hands in hers. "Thank you for telling us this."

"I think these two should go home and forget Edrick, St. Croix, and those ashes."

That suits me just fine, thought Marla. Except, I will never forget St. Croix, Edrick, the ashes, the lovely people I've met here... She looked at Vern and despaired as she recognized the steely resolve in his eyes. She feared he was just getting started on his quest.

They parted and went to their own cars. As Marla was getting into the back seat, she noticed a Chevy Silverado, its right front fender hanging, prowling slowly in the next parking area. The driver turned his head away after their eyes made contact, but in that instant she recognized both the sinister face and the Yankees baseball cap.

Clemma Joseph

The Herbert Grigg Home for the Aged was a short distance from the shopping center. Marla alerted Rosalie to the Silverado and they drove instead toward Christiansted to lose Sammy. He dogged them. When they turned, he did. When Rosalie went through a light as it was changing, he went through the red light. He didn't try to hide that he was following them. Finally, she pulled into a strip mall parking lot and got out of her car. Vern went with her as they waited for Sammy to reach them and pull into the lot. Instead, he tipped the brim of his hat, shifted into neutral, gunned the engine, engaged the clutch, and roared off.

"Son of a bitch." Vern's blurted curse was lost in Sammy's smoky exhaust. He looked at Rosalie and said, "Pardon my French, but what the hell is he trying to do?"

Rosalie assured him. "You don't have to worry about your French around me. I grew up in Newark, New Jersey."

Marla came out of the car and joined them at the edge of the lot. "What's up with that guy?" she asked.

Rosalie led the group back to the car and they settled back in. "I guess you'd call it intimidation in Delaware." She turned her head quickly but not before Marla noticed a flicker of fear in her eyes.

"Do you think he's threatening us?" Marla thought back of Hendrix and how Seymour had told him she was no Obeah woman. She hadn't known the meaning at that time, but now the term was ominous. "Do you think word has gotten out that we had these ashes and maybe someone thinks we really are here to get some Obeah vengeance?" She remembered the night of her mother's dream and how the box seemed to glow from within the backpack. "Maybe the ashes do have some magical power." Marla was not one for superstition, but she firmly believed some inexplicable things just happened, and she found herself considering that they were in over their heads.

Vern turned to face her. "Marla, don't go there. This is getting a little over the top now." His stern look challenged her as he continued. "OK, there have been some amazing coincidences with all of this, but let's not get into voodoo now." He looked to Rosalie for assurance. "Surely people here don't really believe in that stuff, do they?"

Marla gripped the back of Vern's seat, hoping Rosalie would assure them it was all foolishness.

Rosalie's eyes were on the Hospital Street traffic. Workers were returning to their jobs after the long lunch break and the cruise ship tourists were in the center of Christiansted, browsing through shops, not paying much attention to traffic, not looking to their right as they crossed streets. As they turned onto Company Street to begin the journey to the nursing home, she avoided answering at first. Hesitatingly she stumbled through an explanation. "Actually some people do believe it. It's not especially a Crucian thing, but you have to realize a great majority of people here come from all over the Caribbean. Of course that includes Haiti, a real hotbed of Obeah activity, even now in this day and age." She glanced repeatedly in the rear view mirror, and as she did, Marla also looked back to see if Sammy had picked up their trail again.

"Do you believe in it?" Vern asked.

"Let's say I have a healthy regard for its effects."

They rode silently through town and toward the nursing home, each deep in his own thoughts. Marla was frightened and wondered if the fear in Rosalie's eyes mirrored her own. Vern's silence worried her. What had she gotten them all into?

She watched the innocent tourists, completely unaware of the drama playing out in their car, having the vacation of their dreams in the tropical paradise that was becoming unsettling for them with the addition of the Obeahman complicating things. She shook off the worries and bolstered her courage with the renewed belief in her original search. She knew she was destined to find the owner of the ashes, and she had. Whether it was by some divine will or plain detective work, they were here with Edrick's ashes and she looked forward to seeing a mother re-united with her son. Only then would she feel like her mission was completed.

As they turned onto the dirt road leading to the home, Marla saw a mahogany sign carved by the familiar hand. *The Herbert Grigg Home for the Aged*, it said, the *A* in *Aged* the same as in Edrick's *Allawe*. "Edrick, you're home," she whispered.

Eulalie's red Jeep was parked near the entrance. They pulled in next to it, unfolded themselves, stretched, straightened their clothing, and walked toward the front door. The cement buildings were painted in gay colors: a low, bright purple wall surrounding the complex, with a canary yellow border of decorative ridged cement over the lime green supports. The main building was a neutral beige with arched yellow columns resembling the arcades of the main towns on the island. Murals of beach scenes adorned the walls.

"What a pleasant place this is!" Marla thought of the home her mother had been in before she brought her to her townhouse and how drab and dreary it had been.

"It was pleasant even in its early stages." Rosalie pointed to a building that looked ready for demolition, its plaster nearly gone from years of buffeting storms. The metal louvered windows were closed tightly and the hurricane shutters secured. The staircase leading to it was like Eulalie's, only a smaller version with eight shallow steps leading to its main entrance. A gentle breeze whispered through the tall dry grass on the grounds and the pods of the tamarind trees clacked together, tasty wind chimes. "It's designated as an historic building, built in the late 1700s when the Danish were here. They haven't decided whether to let it decay and die or to restore it, so here it sits." They could see a door that had loosened from its hinges, hanging awkwardly on one wall. Rosalie directed their attention to another brightly painted building on the lot. "That's a craft center both for the elderly and local groups." Benches were strategically placed under Norfolk pines and tamarind trees.

Eulalie Williams came out of the home and called them to join her. Marla thought of Whitney Houston everytime she saw Eulalie, her slender figure graceful and tall. She was carrying a shopping bag. "You're right on time." She opened the bag and removed the box. "I think you should present it to her." She handed it to Marla. "My husband's inside. We both thought since you came so far and did so much work, you'd like to actually share the experience with her and with us."

Marla was touched deeply. She looked at Vern and then Rosalie, as if for support. With tears starting to well, as they always did when she was feeling sentimental, she thanked Eulalie. "I'm honored to do this, but do you think she'll accept it from me?" She hadn't expected to actually present the ashes, had just been happy to be there when Ms. Joseph received them. It overwhelmed her.

"Of course she will."

They met Raymond Williams in the visitors' lounge. He was an avuncular man, a little portly, light-skinned, pleasant; he somewhat resembled and even sounded like James Earl Jones. The five proceeded to Clemma Joseph's room. "I've already told her she has a special visitor. She's in good spirits and was trying to guess who it could be."

They passed bright prints that had been painted and drawn by residents, current and past. Scenes of marketplaces, men fishing, children playing in schoolyards. Still, the beauty of the place could not wipe away the antiseptic smell, the odor of aged skin, the traces of incontinence that was the bane of old age. When they arrived at Clemma's room, Eulalie and her husband went in first. Shortly, they called the three into the room. Eulalie had arranged for the roommate to be out of the shared living space.

Marla tentatively stepped into the room. When she saw the woman, so black she was almost blue, she felt a thrill like falling in the dark. Clemma Joseph was silhouetted against the pale wall, sitting up with her stark white sheet pulled up over her lap. Her pink nightgown with the white lace collar accentuated her darkness. The woman's curious eyes were like those of a bird reflecting the flash of a photographer's bulb. Her eyes searched Marla's, reaching out and probing. She spotted the box Marla was holding and the lights in her eyes flashed brighter, almost audibly popping.

Trembling, she pushed the sheet from her lap and drew her legs over the side of the bed.

"Careful, Mama." Eulalie rushed to her side and took her arm.

Marla advanced, holding the box out toward the woman, trying to reach her before she could get out of the bed. But Clemma Joseph rushed at her like a mother dashing to pull a child to safety. Eulalie supported her as the two met. "My son, my son, my son." She took the travel-worn box and kissed it, held it to her bosom, kissed it again, and leaned against her daughter.

Eulalie helped her back to her bed. Clemma removed the lid and inspected the contents. Questions poured out from her expression. She looked at the trio of visitors and back at her daughter and son-in-law. "Where did you find him?" Her aged black fingers, leathery and ashy, paused over the barnacles. "Where has my Edrick been? Who opened this box?"

Her daughter motioned to Marla to remain quiet. "Mama, this is Marla. She lives in Delaware. The box washed up on the beach there and she tracked it down to bring it back to you."

"Delaware? Did that devil Sammy take him back there?" She clutched the box and pulled the sheet up over it, drawing her knees up and hunching her shoulders as she did this.

"Sammy?" Eulalie shot a bewildered look at the others. "Who is he? What does he have to do with this?" She looked at the group and said in a low voice, "Sometimes she becomes a little irrational, imagines things."

Marla moved closer to Vern at the mention of Sammy's name. They looked at each other and Vern's left eyebrow lifted as he drew in a slow breath through his flared nostrils.

"I can hear you, you know." Clemma looked suspiciously at her daughter. "No one ever asked me anything, but I was there. I know they murdered my boy. And now he's back. He'll tell me why." She began to cry. "As if there's a why. As if anybody had any reason to kill my Edrick."

Marla knew Vern's wheels were turning, that the hatred he was already forming for Sammy was intensifying just as her fear was deepening. Her stomach was churning and sweat poured out despite being in the air-conditioned room. The joy she felt when she first presented the box to Clemma turned into a tight anxiety that intensified as she watched Vern.

Raymond had gone out to summon a nurse when Clemma first became agitated. When he returned with her, the nurse steered everyone out except

Eulalie. Raymond led them into the hallway. He explained to them that the police hadn't questioned Clemma after Edrick's body was found. Mervyn had immediately called a doctor who put her under heavy sedation and she was incoherent during most of the time after Edrick's death and memorial service. They all believed she had snapped, especially when she carried the ashes everywhere and searched endlessly after losing them. "But my mother-in-law was always a very sharp woman. It was a stretch to think she'd completely lost her mind. We all thought the death was so devastating that her reasoning was gone. She wasn't able to speak for months after Edrick..." He straightened a print on the wall and examined it. "This print was done by Clemma after she came here."

Marla looked at it and recognized it as the LEAP.

"Not the work of someone who's lost her mind," Vern said; then he looked more closely, pointing to a figure inside the workshop with a snake tattoo running down his arm. "Has Ms. Joseph done any other work that's hanging here?"

Marla stepped closer to the painting and cringed inside as she recognized the Ophi character.

"I don't know. They change the works from time to time. I don't know if even she knows if other drawings of hers are hanging out here."

Eulalie came from the room and joined them. They were still looking at the print. "I always knew Mama was talented. She used to paint and draw a lot in her younger days." She admired the artwork. "We think that is where Mervyn and Edrick got their artistic talent." She raised her eyebrows and studied the print some more. "You can see she still has it. They held an art show over by you, Rosalie, at the clinic on Strand Street. Two of her pieces were on display." She moved away from the print and continued to admire it from a distance. "Every time I see this one, I'm amazed that Mama knew so many details of the LEAP."

"How is she now?" asked Marla. "Was it the right thing, I mean, to bring the ashes here? I didn't want to upset her."

"Definitely the right thing. The nurse gave her a sedative to relax her. But I think she's come alive again." Rosalie smiled. "This is the most alert I've seen her in a long time." She paused before continuing, "Even if she thinks Edrick's ashes will talk to her."

"That may not be as farfetched as you think." Vern addressed the group and pointed to the picture. "Do you know anything about this character in her drawing?"

Eulalie and Raymond examined it closely but came up with nothing. Eulalie said, "I think it's just Mama's imagination. Edrick loved that workshop and carving. Sometimes she'd mutter 'Obeah' out of nowhere. Supposedly snakes are associated with Obeah practices in some places." Her finger tracked the serpent. "Maybe she thought his death was associated with the LEAP and Obeah."

"Did the police ever question her?" Vern asked.

"As I told you," Raymond said, "she was heavily sedated. Since she wasn't actually at the scene of the crime, the police figured they couldn't get anything helpful from her. She was so grief-stricken, plus they had found the body miles from Mervyn's home, so they left her alone."

Rosalie cut right to the chase. "Do you know who killed Edrick?"

Eulalie and Raymond looked shocked by the question. "No, we don't. Neither does Mervyn."

Eulalie's refusal to look into their eyes as she said this made Marla wonder if she knew more than she was saying. She wanted to probe further but was relieved when Vern asked about Clemma's artwork. "Could we see some more of her drawings and paintings?"

"Be my guest." Eulalie led them to the front desk and inquired about the art the residents produced. They were directed to the outlying building, the crafts center, where many works were displayed.

Marla instantly recognized Clemma's work. "Look, another picture of the LEAP." She remarked how her style was similar to VanGogh's rude sketches of the people of the Borinage, the dark colors, the honest laboring. She saw a carver at work, his eyes directed upward as though inspired. She gasped as she noticed the disturbing figure crouching by a wooden barrel, his face hidden by a baseball cap. The letters on the cap were twisted and obscured but surely were Clemma's impression of the New York Yankees logo.

"I think that's the Sammy your mother mentioned." Vern pointed the figure out to Eulalie.

"I don't know any Sammy."

"I'm surprised," said Rosalie. "Many people on the island know him, including your mother and, I imagine, Edrick."

She repeated the name several times, looking at her husband as if he could jog her memory. He provided the key. "Sammy Abramson, Eulalie. The thug who likes people to think he's an Obeahman." He glanced at Vern. "Do you think he had something to do with Edrick's murder?"

"From these drawings, yes, I think he was involved or knows something about it," Vern said.

Marla noticed the firm set of his jaw again and knew his hatred for Sammy was growing stronger. She wished that Saturday would hurry, two more days before they could leave the island and resume their mundane lives. Boring and mundane were looking more and more appealing.

"Are you with the police?" Eulalie took a new look at the visitors. "Did those ashes really wash up on the beach, or have you followed some kind of a lead from Edrick to St. Croix for another reason?"

Now Rosalie was having to play the go-between as Seymour had at the LEAP. "It's incredible, I know, but really - they are telling the truth." She told them about Sammy at Ohna's and how he trailed them. "That's how they came up with his name." She pointed to the drawing. "And your mother identified him both by name and these drawings." She explained how the one inside depicted Sammy's partner.

"Should I call the police?" Eulalie asked, the lines around her mouth and between her eyes etching a formidable grimace. "Mervyn told us that when they found his body, it looked like an Obeah murder, but I never knew of a connection between him and this pair." She looked more closely at the rendering of the mysterious figure in the painting. "This is clearly Edrick in the center, but I never noticed the other man until you pointed it out."

"Can you wait until tomorrow before calling the police? I have the State Police in Delaware checking it out," said Vern. "We don't want to tip Sammy and Ophi off that we have any ideas about them, so how about if we give it some time?"

Shark Attack

They returned to Frederiksted and left Rosalie at her shop. The two played tourists and spent the rest of the afternoon at the Sprat Hall Plantation, a stately bed and breakfast that had originally been a prominent sugar cane operation. They strolled through its grounds, relaxing. "This is where I want to have my birthday party." Vern made reservations that would include his dive friends, Rosalie, and the Williamses. "I wonder if we could spring Clemma free for an evening."

"I doubt it, unless you have a birthday lunch."

"I don't know if that could work. After all, these people are workers not tourists." He asked the reservationist if he could call later to verify a time. "Actually I'd like to know how Clemma's dealing with her son's ashes." He grinned and added, a little mockingly, "If he told her anything."

Marla elbowed him. "Maybe they did tell her something useful." She took his hand as they stood outside the sugar mill; her whole essence tingling and causing a vibration through her body. "This trip has been a spiritual thing for me. Seeing her with that box made me soar," she said. His hand became a tether, keeping her grounded. "I wish we hadn't discovered Edrick was murdered, though. And I'm really puzzled by this whole Sammy thing. Why would he want to scare us?"

"Maybe he thinks we know more than we do. Remember, even Eulalie asked us if we were with the police." Vern pointed to a mongoose scampering across the trail. "Seymour told us 'Mongoose king of de day, rat king of de night.' I think we've come across two giant rats."

Marla was surprised Vern had heard anything Seymour had said on that ride back from the LEAP when he was so fixated on anything outside the van and was steaming in anger with her.

"Babe, you started all of this and kept it going, but I don't think the job is finished yet." They walked down the hill past the bright yellow flowers of the Ginger Thomas trees and flaming reds and purples of the bougainvillea. Marla suspected that, unlike her, he wasn't taking in any of the scenery. She could see that his mind was hot on the murder. What had started as a fantasy as far as he was concerned had become a concrete search, *his* mission. "I want to nail those bastards," he said.

"What if they didn't have anything to do with it?

Vern, we aren't detectives. We don't have any proof."

He stopped in the path and turned to her. "You didn't have any more proof that the box was from here than I have of their guilt. But I'm just as convinced as you were that they either killed him or ordered the murder." He recounted the drawings and Clemma's immediate suspicion that Sammy had taken the ashes back to Delaware, the scene of the crime. "That's proof enough for me." His eyes darkened. "That's more evidence than yours." He mimicked her words in a singsong voice: "'It was a mahogany box and Barney's worker came from St. Croix...'"

The words stung, and Marla became silent. She looked down at the ground and resumed the walk on the path, her hand no longer in Vern's.

"I hope Darryl's cousin comes up with something." Vern didn't appear to notice the effect of his harsh rebuff and picked up the strand he was pursuing.

Marla knew he was right about her scanty information and how she had taken on the search with a leap of faith. She had been so happy with the renewed love she was feeling that she didn't want to jeopardize it. She swallowed her pride and tried to reason with Vern. "But isn't it possible that Clemma was just off her noggin, so to speak?"

"Clemma's drawings are not those of a nutcase. I think her intuition is every bit as sensible as yours." He smiled down at her. "Boy, I'll sure never doubt you again. And I have faith in her observation, too."

She took his hand and again hoped Saturday would come fast. After all, how much damage could be done by then? Once they were safely back at home, Vern would pick up where they'd left off and this mad adventure would be history. Surely he wouldn't want to conduct a search for the murderer from their complex.

As Vern left the Frederiksted pier for his final dive, Marla was tasked with confirming the birthday plans for the next day. The dive crew had a morning and night dive scheduled for Friday, so they agreed an afternoon would be perfect. Marla stood at the pier and waved to the departing boat. They would slowly make their way to the dive spot and take in the setting sun as part of the experience. Marla remembered the thrashing of the sharks at the watergut and intoned a silent prayer as the group pulled out.

On her way back to Rosalie's she noticed a Silverado parked near the shop, close to the place where the truck had nearly hit her. She saw the right fender hanging and stopped in her tracks. Her mouth dried, and her heart raced as she carefully crossed over to Rosalie's shop. Her tongue was glued to the roof of her mouth and her skin paled.

Rosalie rushed over to her as she entered the shop. "You look like you've seen a ghost. What's the matter?"

"S-Sammy." The name stuck in her throat.

She led Rosalie outside and pointed to the truck. They looked across the street at Vern's departing boat and saw a small white motorboat slowly putting out to sea. The boat followed in the wake of the *Scuba Does*. The motorboat was still close enough that they could read its name: *Obatala*. "That's a strange name." Marla's voice had returned.

"Very strange indeed. It's a powerful name in Obeah." Rosalie frowned at the scene. "Does Vern have his phone with him?"

The sight and sound of the snapping sharks came back and Marla reached inside her handbag. She hit the speed dial for Vern. "I hope they're not out of range of the cell tower."

"Hi Babe, what's up?" She could hear the steady putter of the engine in the background. "You're breaking up."

"Sammy's following!" She shouted loud enough to nearly be heard without the telephone, but the connection was lost. She looked frantically at Rosalie and began to cry. "I don't know if he heard me."

"Let's go over to the other dive shop. Bob should have an emergency radio onboard. They'll call him." The dive shop was at the other end of town. They raced there in Marla's car. "Careful now. Stay in the left lane!" she warned.

They double-parked in front of the dive shop and went in. Marla scanned the horizon, but both boats were now out of sight. The owner, Scott Lansing, was alone in the shop. Rosalie quickly told him of the problem and Scott wheeled his computer chair to the marine phone, untangled the flexible cord and put out the distress call over the microphone. "Scuba Does, Scuba Does, this is F'sted Buddy on Channel 9. Over." No response. He tried again. On the third call he heard, "F'sted Buddy, F'sted Buddy, this is Scuba Does on Channel 9. Over."

Scott explained the situation and Bob acknowledged that they knew the boat was trailing them but didn't know who they were. "Well, the little lady Marla is really upset. She says to tell you it's Sammy."

For a moment the radio was silent except for static, and then Bob was back. "Hey, Scott, can you get the Coast Guard out here and ask them to check this guy out for life vests, guns, or something. He's up to no-good, that's for sure. We'll keep an eye out, but we're pretty far out now and if he wants to hurt us, we'll be shark meat and never tell the story." He gave his coordinates and informed Scott that they would not go any farther until the Coast Guard came.

Marla heard the exchange and had to sit down, the roiling waters, snapping rows of razor-sharp teeth, and shark fins whirling again through her head. Sunset turned to darkness as they waited for more word, Marla, standing at the entrance to the dive shop scanning the horizon, looking for lights to appear on the water. The palm trees were black against the moonlit sky, dark sentinels beckoning the sailors to return home. She wanted to hold Vern close to her and never let him go on another dive expedition. She wanted to pack up and go home to Fenwick Island, to their development, to Moliére, to her normal life. She cursed the day she found the box. Then she remembered the lights in Clemma Joseph's eyes, the way she held her Edrick, the love she had for her son. She realized her own mother had loved her the same way but was a prisoner in her mind all those years, that Theresa Collins had been unable to express it, had been too busy making a living and a name for herself. The memory of the night she came to her in the hotel room warmed her. An inner voice stroked her soul and told her Vern would be all right.

An hour passed by, and the inner voice began to waver. She sat in the shop. She stood up and read the posters. And re-read the posters. After the third time she realized she wasn't absorbing anything, that all meaning had escaped. The inside of the shop was suffocating her. Scott's rolling chair irritated her. The wheels squeaked and the leather seat made a rocking noise as he wheeled from the radio to the file cabinet to the desk. She watched him fill the air tanks. Rosalie helped him record the returned fins and snorkels. Marla thought she should offer to help, but she couldn't concentrate on anything. She stumbled into the floor fan and knocked it over.

"I'm sorry." This was all she could manage. She set it upright and went outside. She walked around the small wooden building, picking her way between shells, discarded cans, and racks for diving gear. Music from a bar downtown angered her, making it harder to hear the marine radio inside. When Rosalie went for coffee, she stayed behind, not wanting to miss a call. She ventured onto the beach just yards away from the entrance and sat in the cool sand.

Voices came from the direction of the pier. On the beach, two young men were heading toward her. As the voices grew louder, she gathered her skirt and retreated to the safety of the shop, fear following her every breath and step of the way. Her heart pounded as they turned toward her, but the beat steadied when they passed in front of the shop and went onto the street and into town.

She was afraid that Scott would close the shop for the night, but he refused to leave. It was the code that sailors helped each other. Marla paced between the two wicker chairs and stool inside, sitting on one then the other, to the straight-backed chairs set up at the chessboard outside the shop. She toyed with the chess pieces and watched the horizon. She rubbed the black plastic king and then the white one. She read all the posters again several times, squinting in the light cast by the streetlamp and the moon. The PADI creed: *Teach the value of character and integrity* stood out and she peeked back inside to see Scott finishing paperwork for the day and listening for the radio, waiting vigilantly for a call from the *Scuba Does*. She knew that Scott's PADI flag outside the entrance was well-deserved. Her calm self recognized Bob as a professional, too, but her terrified self knew that Sammy and his cohort were ruthless thugs. Sammy and PADI were not compatible. What was their intent in following the divers? Were Vern and the others safe? Was Sammy just using the tracking as an intimidation method? She prayed, but her thoughts were less than pure. She acquiesced, revised her words and then demanded. *Goddamn it, help them!* and added, *please...* She twisted her ring three times, hoping to bring luck. She thought of her mother. She had told her of a fountain that held a magic ring in Nuernberg, Germany that, when twisted three times, would bring luck. She turned her ring three more times. The moonlight reflected off the diamonds as the ring whirled around her finger.

She heard the radio squawk and rushed inside. "F'sted Buddy, F'sted Buddy, this is Scuba Does on Channel 9. Over." Scott rolled quickly to the desk.

She heard Bob's report. The Coast Guard had radioed ahead for three ambulances to meet them at the pier. They would be pulling in in about fifteen minutes. Everyone was alive but there had been serious injuries. "Vern!" Marla shook Scott's shoulder. "Is Vern OK?"

"He already signed off." Scott apologized and got up from his chair. "The only thing we can do is wait and see. Let's go down to the pier." He locked the shop and all three climbed into Marla's car. Screaming police cars raced past them.

"We may as well park here," Rosalie instructed them. "We won't be allowed any closer."

They were two blocks from the pier. A crowd had already gathered and police were stringing a *Do Not Cross* yellow tape at the entrance to the wharf. One police car pulled onto the dock and the others formed a barricade of flashing red and blue lights around the entrance.

"My husband's on the boat." Marla begged a policeman to let her cross the line.

"And them? What's their business here?"

"Please, they're with me."

She imagined the policeman could see her distress. He waved them through, and they raced to the end of the wharf.

"Here they come!" A shout announced the arrival of the emergency vehicles. The ambulances positioned themselves in the getaway position on the end of the dock and sat with lights flashing, doors open; EMTs ready with intravenous bags, bandages, litters. Nervous tension and excited whispers filled the air as news spread and onlookers appeared from all parts of the town. They pressed against the yellow tape at the far end, but no one crossed the barrier. A police van lurked to the side of the landing, away from the path the ambulances would take.

Marla held Rosalie's arm and huddled against her, shivering in the warm night air. A cold sweat had broken out over her entire body and Scott came over with a blanket from the ambulance. "Here, Marla, put this around you."

"No. No. Leave that for the people on the boat, maybe Vern..." She wound her diamond ring around and around with her thumb and dug into Rosalie's arm.

"He'll be OK," Rosalie tried to reassure her.

"Why would he want to hurt us or anyone?" Marla addressed no one in particular. She spoke as a disembodied voice.

Her question hung in the night sky. Excitement built as the three boats came nearer, the running lights of Sammy's and Bob's boats flickering while the Coast Guard's spotlights flooded the dockside. Commands boomed over the loudspeakers and the injured were evacuated first. Marla scurried to the first litter, then to the second, and watched the boat while others were brought out. The last one carried out was Vern. She ran to his side. "Sorry, lady," a kind West Indian voice warned her to step back and give the workers room to lift the litter into the ambulance. Vern was moaning softly and Marla became frantic when she saw the splotch of blood coagulating on his thin blanket. "That's my husband," she cried. "I need to come with him."

"Sorry, but we have room only for the victims."

"Victims." She swallowed the word and searched the medic's face. "Vern's a victim." Her incoherent eyes and voice glazed over Rosalie, who had caught up to her.

"You can meet us at the hospital." The EMT directed the comment to Rosalie. "Keep an eye on her. I think she'll need treatment, too."

Marla headed for her car, leaving Rosalie standing. Rosalie ran after her, calling out, "Wait for me. I'll drive." Bob was coming off the boat, and as Rosalie took Marla's arm, she pointed to him. "Let's talk to Bob first."

Bob put his arms around both women, and

hugged them close. "It was a nightmare out there. It's good you warned us it was Sammy." He raised his eyebrows, stepped back, and took in a deep breath. "But the divers wanted to get their money's worth and went into the water anyway." His shirt was soaked with blood and his usual grin was gone as he looked around at the chaos on the pier.

Marla watched Vern's ambulance pull away. "What happened to Vern?" She redirected her faltering attention to Bob.

He looked around at the crowd that had gathered. He lowered his voice and told them what Sammy and his partner had done. "At first they just sat there watching. In a way, that gave the divers the idea he was just a crackpot but not a harmful one. I guess he thought Vern was with the rest and they dumped bags of fresh-cut mackerel and bluefish right into where they were diving." He mopped his forehead with the edge of his T-shirt and ran his hand down the side of his face. "Within minutes the sharks were there. We did everything to pull the people out of the water. It was fortunate that they dumped the bait right after the last diver went in. They hadn't gone too deep, so we were able to alert them."

"Was Vern in the water?" Marla was fading, close

to fainting as she listened to the tale. "Why is he so bloody?"

Bob told how Vern jumped out of the boat when he saw what Sammy was doing and swam to him, how he tangled and fought until his partner, Ophi, shot him and pushed him overboard. "Vern was like a madman and he was on the verge of killing Sammy," he said. Bob told how he and the crew were able to get him back into the boat just as a mako was ready to attack. "Right about that time, the Coast Guard arrived and took control."

Marla felt herself slipping away. "Bob, I'm losing her," Rosalie said. She put both arms under Marla's armpits and stopped her descent while Bob helped prop her up.

Marla regained her hold on herself and allowed them to assist her to the car. Onlookers hushed their voices as the trio made their way past them onto the street. They parted, creating a path as she neared the car. A man in the crowd held the back door open while Bob and Rosalie positioned Marla. Then he ran around to the driver's side to guide Rosalie into place. Bob leaned back, exhausted in the seat. Marla said to him, "I'm sorry to cause you so much trouble. You've already been to hell and back." She slumped over in the back seat while

Rosalie and Bob remained in control and drove to the hospital.

"You know, if the Coast Guard hadn't shown up when they did, I think they'd have killed me and the crew and dumped us all overboard. The divers would already have been taken care of by the sharks and we would have been, too." He looked back at Marla. "Who saw them, Rosalie or you?"

Marla couldn't comprehend what he was asking. Rosalie answered for her and told Bob how they had seen the boat trailing them and the aborted phone attempt. Marla sat up in the back seat. The fog had lifted and clarity returned to her eyes. "Are we going to the hospital now?"

They assured her they were and that she could be with Vern. Bob warned her, "Be prepared. He's lost a lot of blood and might need a transfusion, but Ophi wasn't the greatest shot in the rocking boat. So I think Vern might be groggy and sore but he'll be OK."

Marla remembered the blood stain on his blanket and hoped Bob was right.

A Night in the Hospital

Marla spent the night in the hospital, hunched in a chair next to Vern's bed. The blood loss was not enough to require a transfusion, but he was kept overnight for observation. Her fingers were sore from turning her ring and scratching the diamond edges against her skin. She awoke several times through the night whenever she heard his moans. One time she leaned over the restraining bars and held his uninjured side as she could see him replaying the fight with Sammy. "My darling, how brave you were," she whispered.

A nurse entered the room. "Is he awake?" she asked. She stood next to Marla and watched Vern toss in his sleep. "We might need to tie him down so he doesn't do any harm to himself," she said as she saw his rampaging was happening in a nightmare. "If it's any consolation, the other guy is pretty banged up, worse than your husband."

News had spread through the hospital of the

events onboard the dive boat. Vern was already gaining a reputation as a hero and Sammy and Ophi as the thugs that they were, but this provided no consolation to Marla. "Are the others in this hospital, too?"

"The one who tangled with your man is, and the other is in Golden Grove, locked up for now." Marla and the nurse watched as Vern quieted, the fight finished for the time being, as he lapsed back into a drugged sleep. "If he gets too riled up, push this button. I know you don't want him tied, but it might be the best thing for him." She touched Marla's arm, straightened Vern's sheets, left the room, and resumed her rounds.

Vern woke up as the sun's rays streamed into the room. Marla rubbed the sleep out of her eyes, when she felt him shift. She had slouched over the edge of the bed by his feet and fallen asleep there. He opened his eyes and looked at her, confusion written all over his face.

"Happy Birthday, my hero." She leaned over the protective rail and kissed him.

"I bet I have serious bad breath!" Vern must have seen the slight grimace Marla knew she had made.

"At least you have breath." Marla was relieved

they could still make silly jokes in spite of all the trauma. She poured some water for him and held the flexible straw.

"I could use a drink." His dry lips and sour look affirmed it. He craned to survey his bandaged arm. "What's all this about?"

"Bob said Ophi shot you. We're lucky you all came back from this hell."

"If this was the best he could do, they're lucky they came back. Did they?"

She told him what the nurse had said. "I'm glad you made it to your 35th birthday, but I guess you know the birthday party is off."

He struggled to sit up. "What do you mean? I'm leaving here today."

"I think we'd better let your doctor decide that." She looked toward the door, hoping a doctor would miraculously appear, but the hallway was quiet and empty. A voice crackled over the intercom paging a Dr. Warner.

He winced as he supported himself on his right elbow, the heavily bandaged left arm suspended by a pulley system. "That bastard was trying to kill all of us. I'm not going to let him ruin my birthday, too. He already cost me my final dive." His eyes searched the room. "Where are my clothes?"

"Your clothes are pretty bloody. I'll have to get some from the hotel room before you can check out of here, so relax." Marla held the straw in position for him to take another sip. "You beat Sammy up pretty royally. I wonder which room he's in." "All the more reason for getting out of here. I'd like to disconnect him from any plugs first." Vern noticed the tubes coming from his arm and one under the blanket, draining his bladder. "What the hell are all these things they have me hooked up to?" He leaned to the side, straining his injured arm against the pulley and yelped at the pain.

A Voodoo Murder

After receiving advice and a pain prescription from the doctor, Vern checked out of the hospital that morning. The Sprat Hall party was called off, but Rosalie invited them all to her house for a quiet celebration. Bob cancelled both dives for the day, turning them over to Scott. Bob and Vern spent time with the police and Coast Guard, explaining the events of the previous night.

"Wait till you hear this!" he complained when he returned to the room at the Buccaneer. "They told me not to leave the island until this mess is cleared up and they can get the charges in order." He held the slinged limb close to his body with his right hand. "Fine birthday present!" He fumbled for his telephone to notify Darryl and find out what he had learned.

"Don't worry about getting to work." Darryl's excited voice came over the speakerphone. "It looks like you two ace detectives have really hit upon a rat's nest down there." He hesitated briefly. "Seems the guy's murder looked like voodoo or something. They sprinkled corn meal around his body and lab tests showed salt water soaked his shirt."

Marla heard him over the speakerphone.

"Salt water? The closest salt water to Wilmington is probably near Milford."

"Actually they found the body in a Sussex County turn-off at the beach, so Troop 4 is responsible for the investigation. But get this. My cousin, Clint, said the forensics lab showed that this water came from the Caribbean."

"The Caribbean?" asked Marla.

"Yeah, can you imagine that?" Darryl admitted that he was puzzled by that finding.

"Do they have any suspects?" Vern's eyes narrowed as he asked. Marla thought he was visualizing Sammy and Ophi, as she was.

"They probably wouldn't tell me that, but the troopers will want to talk to you and find out what you know."

Marla could visualize Darryl's animated face, but his news about the troopers wanting to talk to Vern was not what she wanted to hear. Even after they returned home, there would be unfinished business, and she wanted it to be over and done with.

"Maybe Sammy and Ophi think we're investigating this case?" she said to Vern and the invisible Darryl. "Do you suppose these guys are stupid enough to think that killing us would stop an inquiry here?"

"This is very much an open case, and the troopers want to get to the root of it. They are pretty sure it's a voodoo murder and don't want that kind of a thing getting a hold here. My cousin said he's going to contact someone from down your way from Troop 4," Darryl warned. " He'll tell them about this development. I think I'd be pretty careful if I were you."

They sat on the terrace, talking about where the trip had led them. "This beautiful place is turning into a nightmare," Marla said. She watched the late morning clouds race through the sky, a particularly windy day, a storm on the horizon. Her thoughts were running rampant. "Surely Sammy and friend are still in custody," she said. But she knew she would not feel safe until she and Vern returned home. "Maybe they thought the case was dead and buried, and our showing up spooked them."

Vern smiled, "Dead and buried? Is that one of your famous puns? Come to think of it, I haven't heard any lately." His wounded arm was resting on the table between them. He held it tightly and she could see the pain pill was already wearing off.

Again Vern displayed that endearing quality Marla admired. In spite of the pain and the difficult situation, he could still find humor.

"I don't know how long they'll hold them – or us for that matter," Vern said. His grim look settled over him and he continued. "I really don't think we can be of any help other than pressing charges against the two for attempted murder, which we did, in fact, this morning. As far as Edrick's murder, I guess I've had enough and just want to go home."

Marla breathed a sigh of relief but knew Darryl was hooked and it wouldn't take much to push Vern back once he went back to work with Darryl. The two were such inveterate gamers. She could just imagine their conversations in the break room at Darryl's office, their computer searches with all the tools they had at their command. Darryl's business, Computer Research, would become Command Center once Vern returned. She shuddered at the thought. If Sammy had gone to Delaware to get Edrick, what would stop him from taking Obeah vengeance on Vern?

The next day would have been their check-out day to return home, but she knew that new details had to be arranged – flight changes, another room reservation, Sybil's availability to continue looking in on Moliére. She was only too happy to start the process. The sooner we get out of here, the better, she thought.

"Let's take a walk up to the front desk, and see what we can do about staying on here," she said. She hoped the walk would take his mind off the pain and that they could enjoy the view from the hotel's terrace again. A cocktail and a rest at the bar with its panoramic view could be just what the doctor ordered. The look on Vern's face when she suggested it made her change her mind. "Maybe a ride to the office would be better," she said. He agreed .

At the reception they were informed there were no available rooms, so they settled for the drinks on the patio and contemplated plan two. "I'm calling Rosalie to see if she knows anyone who can get us a deal," Marla said.

The Birthday Party

The best deal I can think of," Rosalie offered up, "is for you two to stay at my place until you're released. Furthermore, the police should negotiate with the airlines since they're forcing you to stay here. You shouldn't have to pay any additional change fees." It was settled. The two women discussed the plans for Vern's birthday party while he sipped his piña colada and took in the view.

That afternoon they made their first trip to Rosalie's home, following her from her shop, a convoy including Bob and his crew, along with Eulalie Williams and her mother and husband. As expected, Rosalie's house was elegant. Marla couldn't imagine Rosalie in anything other than classy. Sheltered in the hillside over St. George's Botanical Gardens, it was an arboretum in its own right. Rosalie's shop assistant and her husband were there to greet the entourage. So were the three dumpster dogs, who, after sounding the warning of approaching visitors, lapped at Rosalie and wriggled under the petting they begged from Vern and any others they could persuade.

They entered the great hall first, an atrium with a gargoyle- bedecked fountain, squirting water into the center of the display. Marla thought of her mother's description of the Trevi Fountain in Rome and wondered if it could be as magnificent as this one. She had never seen a fountain in someone's home. Seating arrangements encircled the fountain, small conversational groupings of four seats from ottomans to wicker and rattan chairs surrounding glass-topped, Italian ceramic, and wicker tables. It seemed that each grouping represented a corner of the globe. She leaned against Vern's good arm and whispered, "Wow, is this real?"

Vern looked into her eyes, the flecks picking up all the highlights from the lime dress she'd bought at Rosalie's. "No, I think we're in heaven. Did that shark get me?"

They all inspected Rosalie's home. She gave them the grand tour and showed Marla and Vern the room they would occupy until they returned to the States. "Pretty elegant, if you ask me." Vern was impressed with the four-poster bed, the teak armoire, the doors of all the bedrooms opening onto a center court, the vegetation, the magnificence of Rosalie's entire home. "We'll never be satisfied with our two tiny bedrooms in

Delaware, after this."

"Well, don't forget the Gannet Hardware job I told you about," Eric reminded. The entire group was being led on the tour and all were impressed.

Bob brought them back down to earth. "I don't think that job will buy you a place like this."

The birthday dinner was served in Rosalie's dining room at a table large enough to seat fourteen guests, although only nine were present. A side table was heaped with island specialties: conch, baked fish, local lobster known as langouste, seasoned rice, pigeon peas, and side provisions of boiled plantain, lettuce, and tomatoes. Bright foil Happy Birthday balloons hovered over all. Diarra, Rosalie's assistant, ran a catering business with her husband, and they proudly stood by while toasts were made to Vern's health; they joined in with the well-wishing.

"Speech, speech!" demanded Bob.

Vern reached into his sling and brought out a rolled-up scroll. He let it drop open and as it reached his knee, he began with a senatorial voice, "I didn't expect to have to address you all today." He was unable to go with the joke and let the scroll fall to everyone's howls of laughter. Then he continued, "Seriously, I'm just happy to be alive in this beautiful place with all of you." He reached out with his right arm and beckoned Marla to stand beside him. Together, the two faced their well-wishers. "Rosalie, how can we thank you for your hospitality and help? Bob and the *Scuba Does* crew, what can I say? Eulalie and Raymond, thank you for letting us share in your mother's precious moment. And Ms. Joseph..." Marla went to her seat and escorted her to the head of the table. He continued, "You're the reason we're here."

The crowd applauded as Clemma hobbled to the head table, carrying her son with her. She smiled at the group and caressed the box. "Thank you for bringing him back to me. Now le' we eat 'fore someone come and tief all dis good food!" Applause broke out again at her call for eating before someone could steal the food.

This was just what everyone wanted to hear and they formed a line at the side table, Clemma Joseph going first followed by the birthday boy. "I'm so glad they let you come here today. This is very important to me." He assisted her with her plate, as best he could with one arm, and seated her at the head of the table before going back to help himself.

"I feel alive again," Marla heard her whisper into his ear before he left her side.

Dinner conversation was spirited and filled with stories of their narrow escape. The dive crew toasted Vern again and again, saluting his efforts to rub out Sammy, Marla's warning, the fast action of the crew in pulling the divers literally from the jaws of the sharks. "We're lucky that nobody was killed. Evie might lose her arm, but the other three only lost tanks and flippers. And a little blood..." Bob shook his head repeatedly as he relived the horror-filled minutes. "Like you, Vern, I'm glad I'm here!"

Everyone at the table was sobered by the line of conversation. Bob ended it with, "Well, let's just hope that Evie recovers and that the others get over the shock. And that Sammy and Ophi are put away." He lifted his wine glass and proposed another toast. "And let's hope that Vern and Marla return here many times!"

"If we're ever allowed to leave!" Vern laughed and accepted the toast.

"How were you able to warn the divers?" Marla had been curious about that since the incident occurred. "And was Evie the farthest down or something? How did the shark get her arm?"

"You're sharp." Bob directed a toast at Marla. "We banged like hell with a wrench on the metal ladder. We had briefed them beforehand, a common practice, like a flight attendant giving crash precautions." He blanched when he talked about the last diver, Evie. "She got in the way of one of the makos. They were busy gobbling down anything in the water. And she was the last one up."

The Williamses left before the others as they had promised the nurses they would have Clemma back before dark. "She wants to go back to Mon Bijou, to her house." Eulalie told Vern and Marla that Clemma had remembered something Edrick had told her before he left for the States, something that had been nagging at her since the return of the chest. "My mother has a strong will. Having Edrick back has given her a strength we haven't seen in a while." She directed a smile at her mother. "We're taking her over there for a short visit tomorrow."

"Be sure to stop by and say hello to Miss Anna." Rosalie told them how concerned the pleasant woman was and of her good wishes.

The remaining group lingered over dessert and after-dinner drinks and made plans for the move the next day from the Buccaneer. John, the other crew member, offered the use of his beater car if they couldn't extend the car rental.

"Well, my arm is starting to throb, so I guess that means it's time for us to leave." Vern held the arm close to his side and stood up. "I hate to break up this wonderful party, but is anyone else leaving soon?" He looked toward Marla. "I'm not sure we can find the way out. Can we?"

The others rose and Bob agreed to lead the way. "We need to go, too. Remember boys, we have dives tomorrow!"

Bob led the group down through the hills and winding dirt roads. The bush hugging the sides of the road was thick and tall. At some stretches, trees overhung the road and joined in the center, forming an arched thoroughfare. As pre-arranged, Bob shot his arm out the window and pointed to landmarks that would help them find their new home the next day. At one turn it was a dumpster next to a small galvanized shack. At another it was a huge flamboyant tree, now flaming red but soon to lose its bright color. A third landmark was a rutted intersection, one rut clearly dominating and leading to Rosalie's. They came to Centerline Road. Marla sounded the horn and Vern thrust his good arm out the window with a hearty wave.

A Little Beach Area on

Coastal Highway

On Saturday morning, Vern stopped at the doctor's office to have his arm checked. After a review, the doctor re-applied the bandage and pronounced him fit. "You're lucky there was no nerve damage. This is going to be sore for a while and you'll need therapy, but you should have a full recovery."

"How about the others from the dive boat?"

"Well you know I can't give out that information, but you can visit the only one still in the hospital and ask her yourself."

Things weren't so different from practices in the States. The doctor continued, "The others were all released the same night."

"Including Sammy Abramson?" Vern hoped the doctor would shed some light on that topic.

"That one is in Golden Grove now, along with his partner. I don't imagine you'll want to visit him." The Filipino doctor told him that he was aware of all that had transpired that night. His office in the hospital had been visited by police the day after the incident. A crime on the territorial seas was not taken lightly, and it seemed Sammy was in for more trouble than he'd bargained. "I think they're going to transport them to a more secure prison sometime next week."

As they walked down the corridor toward Evie's room, Marla wondered what a "more secure prison" meant. Were they locked up tight enough for now, until she and Vern could leave the island? "I don't trust this a bit. What if he gets out and comes for you again?"

"Let's hope he doesn't know we're at Rosalie's. But really, what are the chances he can both escape prison and then find us?"

Marla was mollified by Vern's assurance. She looked at room numbers and found Evie's room. She poked her head through the door and made eye contact with the young woman. Her right arm was elevated and encased in bandages that could have hidden a body between her shoulder and wrist. She managed a broad smile as the two entered the room. "Are we the worst casualties?" she asked Vern.

"It looks like it. Evie, this is Marla, my wife. Marla, Evie." The two moved close to her side. "Has the doctor visited you today?" He grimaced as he examined the huge bundle of gauze and surgical wrap.

"He was here early. They re-attached what was hanging and think there's a good chance it will take. I understand I was in surgery for fifteen hours." She shifted a bit, watching to see if her arm moved. "I have to be really careful."

"I'm sure," said Marla. "Can we help you in any way?"

"Yes, make it all go away. It's so unreal. Thursday was my first day of vacation, and it looks like I'll spend the whole holiday in this great spa." She looked around at the amenities: a plastic bedpan, remote control for the wall-mounted TV, plastic drape separating her bed from her roommate's, the bare green walls, all accented by an antiseptic smell that permeated the room and hallways. "And of course my whole package took me months to save for... Everyone says I should just be grateful to be alive. And of course I am."

She adjusted herself again with her left arm and sat more upright. "What happened anyway? Bob's been here a time or two but I was pretty much out of it."

Vern recounted Thursday night's events. He

poured her a glass of ice water, and Marla went to the gift shop to get a magazine for her. Evie shuddered at the telling of the story; thankfully the human brain has a way of deleting the most horrific details from such an experience, and she listened as though he were telling someone else's story.

When Marla returned, they rigged up a system so Evie could read the magazine and lay it on the bedside table with her left hand when she got tired. Marla promised her before they left, "I'm not sure how much longer we'll be here, but we'll be back to visit you."

They began their journey to Rosalie's, their bags packed, ready for the flight they couldn't take. "I'm glad I can drive stickshift," Marla said. They had stopped at the car rental after leaving the hospital and picked up what John called his beater car. The back floor had a hole much like the one in Seymour and Owin's van. "Besides the wobbly gearshift, this Crucian air conditioning system is fun, too." Marla adjusted the rearview mirror. "What time do the police want to talk to you again? We may end up walking to Christiansted."

"Not until after lunch on Monday. That leaves today and tomorrow for being tourists. I hope we can leave Tuesday." She watched Vern study the highway, looking for familiar landmarks. They passed the high school and university with its palm lined entrance and then saw a low group of buildings surrounded by concertina wire. "That looks like the minimum security prison in Georgetown."

Marla agreed it resembled their local prison in Delaware. A sign identified it as the Golden Grove Correctional Center. "Oh no, he's right in our neighborhood." They were both familiar enough to know that the turn-off to Rosalie's would be coming soon.

"Well, I hope he's still hurting from the beatdown. Not to mention that I hope he can't escape from there." Vern's face had its pondering look, his lips screwed up as he deliberated. "I can't figure out why he hates me – us – so much that he would kill me and that entire crew. What does he think we know? And how would killing us remove any threat?"

"Either he's just plain stupid, or those ashes held some secrets he didn't want dredged up." Marla concentrated on staying in the correct lane and making the turn toward Rosalie's. "Was it just chance that he was at Ohna's that night, or had he been following us and we didn't know it?"

Vern's phone rang. He fumbled with his good arm, pulling at his pocket and straining against the seat belt. He couldn't reach it. When Marla pulled to the side, he saw that it was Darryl who had called and he called him back. Marla watched Vern's face as he talked, his eyes growing narrow with what she thought might be worry or concern. When he hung up, he told her that Darryl's cousin said an investigator from Troop 4 had booked a flight for Monday and wanted to talk to local police on St. Croix. "They think Sammy and Ophi might be connected with the murder in Delaware and might want to seek extradition."

Marla pulled away from their parking space and resumed their trip. "What makes them think it was these two?" she asked.

He reported more of Darryl's conversation that surveillance tapes showed three men, two of them unknown and the third, Edrick, entering the location where Edrick's body was found. They'd had a tip that some drug transfers had taken place at that little beach area on the bayside of Coastal Highway.

"What are the chances that the two unknowns could be these two thugs? They're taking a shot in the dark since they really don't have anything else to go on," Vern offered. "Darryl said there were possible connections with drug smugglers using Dover Air Force Base, that some of the deals were being handled in Sussex County. They're coordinating with military authorities. Wouldn't it be a real kicker if the two unknowns were our two favorite Obeahmen?"

"Right in our own backyard. Both in Fenwick Island and here!" Marla frowned at Vern. "We could have gone right past the murder taking place!" She shook her head and looked back at the prison, still visible from where they had made the turn to Rosalie's. "And then we could have been in the middle of one here, too! What a small world this is." Her whole body trembled with the thought.

Botanical Gardens

The two continued their journey to Rosalie's and easily recognized all Bob's landmarks. The trio of watchdogs bayed and howled at their arrival, leaping and scratching at the door. Marla found the spare key in the mouth of the cement leatherback turtle that stood guard at the entrance. "Rosalie said we should make ourselves at home," Marla said, pouring rum punch into two glasses. They went with the dumpster dogs to the outside courtyard, where the hounds were all over Vern, sniffing at his wounded arm, surrounding him as they made their way to the rattan chairs by the lap pool.

"I hope they're not this friendly with all the guests, like maybe Sammy," Vern said as he protected his damaged arm from their inquisitive noses.

"There's our room over there." Marla pointed to a bedroom across from them. "I can see the four-poster bed." She counted three other bedrooms in the wings surrounding the courtyard. "I wonder if she ever has a full house here."

Vern   stretched   and   walked   around   the

courtyard, looking in the windows of the guestrooms, accompanied by his newfound faithful herd of dogs. "I wonder if there's a way into this courtyard other than through the house." The courtyard backed into a solid wall of earth, reminiscent of the cave dwellings of the Southwest. Someone would have to parachute in to gain entrance from that part of the complex.

"Now you're scaring me. Why would you ask that question?"

"You saw the jail."

The dogs bounded away from Vern and into the house, barking clipped high-pitched yelps and whining. Marla rushed to Vern's side, shielding his injured arm.

"It's OK. I already understand these mutts. That's their happy sound. I'll bet Rosalie's home.

Rosalie settled her friends into their room and detailed her day at the boutique. A cruise ship had caused a big run on business in the morning, but the afternoon was slow and she closed early to be with her houseguests. She had received a call from Eulalie Williams, inviting the three to dinner that evening. Clemma was staying with them, a possible precursor to her moving back in with them or returning to their home on Mon Bijou. Rosalie reported that Clemma's clarity of mind was remarkable, that she had regained her senses with the return of her son's ashes. Eulalie told her she had some news that would be of great interest to them.

They spent the rest of the afternoon at the nearby Botanical Gardens. Rosalie took them through, explaining some of the history of the island and pointing out the various flowers, shrubs, and trees that were also on her property. Some provided shade, some color, some food, and some privacy. She often consulted with the horticulturists at the Gardens for advice. They roamed the gardens, exploring the sugar mills, surveying the ruins of the ancient Arawak village, along with the foundations and remaining Danish buildings from the past. Marla found herself falling more and more in love with island. In addition to the "island smell," its colorful history and its present character appealed to her artist's soul. "I'm beginning to understand why you've stayed her so long," she confided to Rosalie.

"OK, don't get any big ideas," Vern warned. "As soon as we're cleared, we're going home."

At the words, "we're going home," Marla smiled a secret smile and turned her face so Vern couldn't see it.

Rosalie noticed the way Vern was cradling his arm. "Let's not wear ourselves out. We have a big evening ahead and one last day tomorrow before, hopefully, you get your release from the police."

She pulled at an asteraceae with its delicate lavender flower. "We can cut some of this and make bush tea. We call this the inflammation plant, and I have it in my herb garden. It'll speed up the healing of your arm."

The List

That evening dinner was served in the dining room, looking out at Eulalie's garden. Candles flickered at both ends of the table, along the walkways in the garden, in the wide stone windowsills, and on every occasional table. They lent an enchantment to the house that soothed Marla and almost made her forget the trauma, the danger they had faced, the near loss of Vern. She leaned over and whispered to Vern, "She could serve fried seaweed and this would still be a perfect night."

"In some places that would be a perfect meal."

Marla rolled her eyes and let out a slow breath through her nose.

"This is a specialty of the house," announced Raymond, as he carried out a steaming tray to join the other bowls of food on the table. "Baked dolphin." He stood ready to serve each a portion when Eulalie burst into laughter as she noticed Marla's face turn green.

"Please, Marla, dear. It's not Flipper. It's a dolphin fish."

They all enjoyed the relief on her face and settled

into the meal. The tangy salsa was made from mangoes on their property. Vern ate two servings of everything, to the delight of the Williamses. "We does love to see folk eat," Eulalie said, slipping into Crucian. This use of the language warmed Marla. She thought to herself, we're family now...

Clemma had been quiet most of the evening. Eulalie told them how she had helped prepare the meal. The dolphin recipe was one of her favorites, one that Edrick had loved. Raymond had seared it quickly on the grill, then under Clemma's supervision slathered an herbed butter mixture over it and finished it off in the oven. Marla enjoyed it all the more knowing it was Clemma's recipe. Clemma's cheeks shone with pride and joy, seeming to have filled out and taken on a fresh appearance as she watched her guests take each bite. Marla wondered if the box of ashes, which were nowhere in sight, had taken a back seat now that Clemma had resumed her place as mother of the clan. Looking around the table, she realized this included her, Vern, and Rosalie, and she smiled.

Eulalie cleared the table and turned the conversation over to her mother. "Mama, do you want to tell our guests what you remembered?"

Clemma looked around at each one before

beginning. Marla picked up on the confidence and assurance that was growing in the woman as she began to speak to the gathering. Clemma sat upright, head held high, voice strong. "I believe I've been living in a fog since I lost Edrick, but holding his ashes and having him with me these past days brought back memories of that terrible night." Her face was illuminated by a candle at her place and it made it seem like they were at a séance. "I remember that night Sammy came for him at Mervyn's house. Just Edrick and me, we were alone, in the back room, watching *Wheel of Fortune*, like we always did." Vern leaned forward and Marla caught his change of posture. They were all hanging on every word as Clemma continued quietly. "He answered the door and then came back to me in the bedroom and told me he'd be back in about an hour. He was holding the jewelry box he had made for me. I thought it strange that he told me the box had an important secret." She pushed her chair back and left the table. Eulalie and Raymond were not surprised at her departure, but the others exchanged glances and looked toward their hosts for a hint of what was going on. Clemma stopped in the hallway, turned, and said to the group, "I looked out the window after he left and saw the three of them. I know it was those devils that left with him. It was days later that Mervyn told me they'd found his body. After that news, I think it's safe to say I lost my mind. But it's coming back now."

Marla studied Vern's face as he followed Clemma's retreating back and swelled with love, remembering his loyalty and concern for her mother.

Eulalie assured them she'd be back. "She's going for the box."

She looked older when she returned, holding the box and a narrow metal pin that looked like half a bobby pin. Eulalie helped her settle back into her chair. Clemma placed the box on the table and laid the pin next to it. "He gave me this pin before he left the island and told me this box was very special, and not to lose the key. Before he left for the States, I tried the key on the bottom, but there was nothing inside." She turned the box upside down and showed them where she had scraped the barnacles off. "I had forgotten that there was a lock here at the bottom." She inserted the key and showed them the false bottom. "Here's why Edrick handed me the box before he left with that devil Sammy."

She slid the bottom off to reveal a compartment

at the base of the box.

Eulalie opened a plastic bag with a folded note inside. "It's a list of names. Edrick must have hidden the list in the box. He must have known there would be trouble even before he left," she said.

Raymond added, "Since Mama had the funeral home seal the box, it probably also protected the secret compartment during its voyage."

Marla turned to Vern and said, "Edrick's ashes did talk to her."

The yellow lab under Vern's chair growled and bristled. He lifted his muzzle and let out a series of choppy barks. The other dogs picked up the warning and all raced to the garden area, sounding an alert. Everyone at the table froze. A candle was overturned by a flailing tail and Eulalie quickly picked it up and blew it out. All five dogs ran out to the edge of the garden and escalated their barking. Digger, the smallest but greatest defender, led the others. His ears stood up straight and his wailing bark spurred the other dogs on. Raymond went out to check, carrying a wide-beam flashlight and a .22 caliber rifle. "Who's there?" he called. Vern joined him and they heard footsteps retreating into the tall bush at the back of the garden. The barking slowed and the dogs touched noses and returned to the dining area with the men.

"Probably kids." Raymond explained that there was a shortcut to a banana grove that lay to the west of their house. "Nobody usually is out there at night, but it happens from time to time."

Marla waited at the door and held her arms together, shivering in spite of the warm evening. "You don't think they could have escaped, do you?"

"Let's hope not." Vern seemed as edgy as Marla over the incident and his noncommittal answer did not soothe her. He looked back toward the banana grove and checked the dogs, all five now quiet and back at their places in the house. Although the scene had quieted, Vern told Eulalie and Raymond how insecure the prison looked to them and how they were constantly looking over their shoulders, still seeing Sammy and Ophi at every turn.

Eulalie offered to call a friend to check on the status of the prisoners, but Raymond stopped her. "Maybe we'd better take another look at that list first." He thought one of the names was the warden of the Golden Grove Correctional Institution.

Vern opened the plastic baggie and started to read the list of names. At the fourth name, he stopped. "Here's how Sammy got onto us in the first place."

Marla looked over his shoulder. "Hendrix!" She shuddered at the remembrance of him. "He must have put the word out as soon as we left the LEAP."

There were fifteen names on the list, none but Sammy, Ophi, and Hendrix familiar to Marla and Vern, but the others recognized some of them. The most important name on the list for Raymond was the warden at the correctional center. He pointed it out and said, "They may not have been out back, but you can be sure they'll be on the streets before daybreak. Herman Roberts – there could be others by that name, of course, but there have been several escapes from that center, all under investigation, and all in the middle of the night." He shook his head. "Now I guess we know how it happens."

Marla thought back to Darryl's comments about the murder scene and surveillance of drug activity. "We can't be putting you all in danger." she said. Feelings of guilt assailed her. She had brought so much trouble, not just on herself and Vern but to this entire gathering of such dear friends. She searched Clemma's kind face for a sign of disdain, a rebuke for bringing this upon them. But her pleasant countenance showed no such criticism. Clemma held Edrick's ashes, the strength of them bringing her an inner peace that could not be shattered, and Marla was consoled by this, convinced that her quest had brought more good than evil to the mother.

But what about Rosalie? Sammy might want to harm her for sheltering the two, for being their friend. Did she deserve to have been brought into this? And the Williamses? If Sammy and Ophi had been the source of the noise out back, their lives would also be ruined. What had she done by picking that box out of the ocean and bringing it here?

Rosalie's protective attitude interrupted Marla's thoughts. She seemed to pick up on Marla's distress and came over, hugged her friend close to her, and wrapped her in the warmth that relieved the coldness that had swept over her. "Do you know of a safe haven anywhere on this island?" she asked Eulalie and Raymond. "I think Marla and Vern will feel better if they could disappear a while before leaving St. Croix."

They discussed some possibilities. Since Sammy knew about the friendship with Rosalie, she could also be targeted. With the warden being linked to the case, going to the police was questionable. "It's Saturday night. How about if I call Darryl and see if he can get us any help from his cousin, if there might be something like witness protection here," Vern suggested.

"It won't hurt," agreed Raymond. He looked troubled, a shadow passing over his face. "I wonder if Edrick was in league with these people. What could his connection have been?"

Clemma pushed her chair back and looked fiercely at Raymond. "Edrick would never be friends with Sammy," she said. "When he went away with him that night, I knew something was wrong. I could feel the evilness from Sammy. And Edrick was not evil."

"Of course he was not friends with them," Raymond said as he went to her side and bent down to hold her close.

Marla was touched by Raymond's gentleness and protectiveness toward his mother-in-law. She remembered how Vern had been the same with her mother those last days. Before she had become so ill, her mother would never have accepted consolation or show of caring. How troubled a life Theresa Collins had led. Marla vowed to absorb all the lessons she was learning on this trip and make her life more giving, and more important than that – more accepting. She saw how Raymond seemed to receive absolution from Clemma. Ms. Joseph leaned back into her son-in-law and allowed him to comfort her.

"I'm sorry, Mama," he said. "Of course Edrick wouldn't be friends with any of them, even Hendrix."

Eulalie told them how Hendrix would often try to pass off Edrick's work as his own, but anyone who knew artwork could see the difference between the two men's products. One thing he never tried to do was imitate Edrick's script, so flowing and artistic. Any carver on the island could manage a decent palm tree, but Hendrix would say that Edrick's trees were his when tourists would come to the LEAP; however, if the carvings had words on them, he didn't even try that approach. He had been caught in his deceptive game several times, which had led to confrontations between him and Edrick. Edrick had begun to carve a distinctive *EJ* on the bottom of his pieces so anyone who really wanted one, could tell.

Marla noted that Clemma's lips tightened during the conversation, and she knew as she shook her head that her anger toward Hendrix was growing. She wondered if her mother had ever been defensive of her, if Theresa Collins had ever had reason to challenge anyone on her behalf. Clemma's hands surrounded the box and she looked down at it, protectively drawing it closer.

Vern called Darryl, who was impressed by the discovery of the list and told Vern he'd contact someone from Troop 4 in Delaware and call him back.

The candles that had glowed with such cheer and warmth earlier now seemed to flicker with foreboding. Marla lost herself in her thoughts and sipped the dinner wine quietly, resting one hand on Vern's knee. A breeze caught the candles on the windowsills and played with them, the flames yielding to the pressure that threatened to extinguish them. She noticed the struggle and thought of O. Henry's *The Last Leaf*. Would the candles going out signal their end, too?

Her hand dug into Vern's leg as the phone rang. Mark Allen, the investigator from Troop 4 called Vern and asked him about Marla and Vern's safety. "Well, Vern, it'll be hard for me to contact anyone there," they all heard Mark's voice say, booming on the speakerphone. "I don't have a personal connection with anyone, and on a Saturday night, I don't know who I can get in touch with, either. You're in a tough spot, I have to admit." He asked him to read the names from the list, and he carefully wrote them. "Some of those names are from here in Delaware, in fact right from your neck of the woods. If you could just make yourself invisible, that's what I'd suggest." Mark promised to fly Marla and Vern back with him in a military jet from St. Croix to Dover Air Force Base.

After the call ended, the group was depressed. Raymond directed them into the living room, where they settled into the cushioned chairs facing the terrace. Marla resumed her vigil and noticed the candles were no longer flickering on the windowsills. This eased her somewhat. No one said anything until Raymond offered the after dinner rum and coffee drinks. Then the group perked up a bit and Rosalie offered to help Eulalie. Even though they were all at risk, only Clemma seemed truly content. Vern had closed the box and her son was still intact. "My Edrick, he told us something, didn't he?" she said as she stood up to help with the drinks.

"He sure did, Mama. It looks like he knew Sammy might harm him and he left the names in good hands, didn't he?" Eulalie rubbed her mother's back and hugged her. "Why don't you stay here with Marla and Vern while we make the coffee?"

"The thing I still don't get," said Marla, "is why these thugs think they can get rid of us and that will solve their problem, whatever that problem is. Don't they know that will only bring more heat?"

"I think it's intimidation." Raymond walked to the terrace door and scanned the back garden, the dogs quietly accompanying him. He sipped his rum and coffee. "If he scared you enough, you'd leave. Or, better yet, if he killed you and made it look like shark attacks, nobody would be the wiser. He can't possibly know about the list, so I don't really think he's after that. Remember, he's the big Obeahman. He'd like nothing better than to brag about how he chased you off the island, you being the white devils who brought the dead back here." Raymond put the empty cup on the serving tray and took his rifle back out of the cabinet and rubbed it. "I'll have old faithful right beside me all night. Mama, you're staying here with us, and you folks are all welcome to stay, too."

Rosalie was the first to respond. "That sounds like a great idea, but I have three dogs at home who wouldn't appreciate it if I don't let them out. I'm sure you know how they'd let me know."

Marla wondered whether the bravado Rosalie

was showing was for Marla's sake, that she was trying to minimize the dangers to soothe her. Or whether she really didn't feel at risk. "Don't you think they'll look at your house for us?" asked Marla.

"First they have to escape. After the caper they pulled, I think the warden would really jeopardize his credibility if he let that happen. Next, they'd have to find my house. I have no reason to believe they know where I live," Rosalie explained to Marla.

Their exchange seemed to go unnoticed by Vern, who was looking over the list again. "Hey, Marla, isn't this the guy who owns that sleazy bar near us?"

Marla sat next to Vern and looked over his shoulder at the list. "Perry? That little wimp? The trooper said some were from our area. It's got to be him." She shivered again. "I always knew something was up over there. This is sounding like a major drug investigation to me. Rumors were that local drug dealers were over there all the time." She thought of the grisly murder of Edrick not far from their home, of drug deals, and possible ties to dealers in their own back yard, so far from St. Croix.

"That could account for the offer of a military ride – probably a liaison between federal authorities and state police. It's starting to make a little more sense now," Vern said. He saw the question on Marla's face and went on. "Edrick, undercover, Caribbean drug smuggling, Virgin Islands flying military jets to Dover?" She knew he could see her calculating, sorting out the data.

"OK, so this goes deeper than we thought," said Marla, "but what do we do now?"

She and Vern looked at each other and Vern took the lead. "I guess we hunker down for the night and disappear like Mark said." Apparently he had been listening to Rosalie earlier because he addressed Raymond, "Thank you for the gracious offer, but Rosalie, we're with you and we're sticking to it." He turned to the others. "If they get out, they might not make a connection to you folks, but Rosalie has been with us when he's seen us, and he knows her. If she thinks she should go home, I'm not letting her go alone."

Marla shook her head in agreement, but deep fear showed in her eyes and Clemma noticed it first.

Clemma suggested that they stay the night at the church in Christiansted. If he's the Obeahman he pretends to be, he wouldn't enter a church - ever," she had reasoned.

Marla liked the idea. "I wanted to visit that

church anyway." She did not like the idea of staying overnight at Rosalie's, did not share her confidence. "We could stay overnight and attend services in the morning. Can we call from here to see if it's possible?"

Marla had converted from the Catholic faith and was a zealot at times, like many converts to a different religion. This had been an issue with her mother, but Marla felt very comfortable with her new faith. It was Vern's professed religion, but she was more dedicated to it than he. Good, she thought, a way to get Vern to go to church with me.

"I'd like to see if an Anglican service is different from an Episcopal one."

Vern said, "Marla, I can't believe you want to go church hopping when we may end up as sacrifices on the altar!"

"Now, Vern," she reasoned, "I think Clemma has a point about Obeahmen not wanting to set foot in a church. I think that's the safest haven we could hope for."

Clemma was a member of the congregation and very much loved by the priest and congregants, Eulalie assured them, and she called Father Ambrose. After hearing of the drama surrounding the visitors, he welcomed them to stay at the rectory with him. He guaranteed Eulalie that her friends would be safe in his church. He would be waiting for them that evening.

A Calling Card

The three headed back to Rosalie's house and discussed the next step in their unusual trip. They convinced Rosalie that she should also spend the night at the rectory. She reluctantly agreed and decided the dogs could be left in the courtyard until her return Sunday. "I still don't know why they want to come after you," Rosalie said. " You really don't have anything they need."

"They must think we do," Marla said.

Marla could tell Vern was thinking about the list Edrick had made. He had tucked it into a loose spot in the back cushion of Rosalie's Honda and she saw him fumbling around the opening with his free hand. "There's no way they could know about that list," he said. "If they knew about it, they'd have found a way to get it from Clemma long ago. I think he's just showing he's the big man like Raymond said, and I --- we--- are his to do with what he wants." He looked at Marla. "Fortunately I think he wants me more than you."

This did not console Marla as she re-lived her terror of Sharky's stories at Davey Jones's Locker, the day they saw the feeding frenzy, the night he was on the boat, the night in the hospital when she wasn't sure how he would recover.

"He surely has made it a personal vendetta." Rosalie inspected the bush on the sides of the dirt road as she made her way to the fork, taking the bigger rut carefully, watching the tall grasses as well as the rut. "I hope your Delaware authorities can remove them both from this island for good."

"I hate to say it, but there needs to be something concrete to connect him to Edrick's murder," Vern said. He wasn't convinced they could get a conviction.

Marla was more hopeful. "From what we know of this creep, he's not too smart. We still don't know how Edrick died. Maybe he left a calling card there." She mulled that over while watching the road for any sudden movement in the bush, any blockading of their course.

St. John's Anglican Church

T hey gathered up their few belongings. Marla sat on the edge of the four poster bed. "I really was looking forward to staying here."

"We'll have to come back in the winter for your birthday," he said. "When it's freezing in Fenwick Island, we'll appreciate this even more. Maybe we can stay with Rosalie the whole time." Oliver, the shaggy brown dog who had taken the greatest liking to Vern, whipped his feathery tail as if he knew what he was saying and yipped an affirmative approval.

"As long as you agree not to go scuba diving and as long as Sammy and Ophi are put away." She inched herself off the bed and pulled the chubby little dog toward her, but he was having no parts of her. He wiggled out of her arms and padded over to Vern, stuffing his nose into Vern's sling. "Yeeow." Vern's cry scared Oliver from the room and Rosalie came running.

"No problem," Vern explained as he rubbed his arm. "Just a little puppy love."

"These dogs have really taken to you, especially this one. You'll have to come back when this is all resolved." The three laughed. Then their serious thoughts took over again. Rosalie had packed an overnight bag, fed the dogs, and watered the plants. "We need to take both cars. Then you can stay at the rectory until you've had your appointment and I can come back here tomorrow. If we make it through the night, we'll be OK. I can check with Eulalie tomorrow to see if those two are still in prison."

Marla realized that Rosalie really *did* have a certain amount of fear about the prisoners escaping and finding her home. She watched her check the lock on the sliding glass door that opened into the garden and followed her through the house helping her to check the windows and various entrances into her sprawling home. Rosalie lingered at the imported ceramic table in her atrium, staring at it and stroking her hand across its shiny surface as though she might not see it again.

Vern argued that they should all go in John's beater car. Sammy could never make a connection to it, and since he obviously had been tracking them, he probably knew Rosalie's Honda. Marla drove and Vern sat in the front with her. They decided Rosalie would be better able to avoid the hole in the back floor than Vern with his one arm. With no moonlight to illuminate the dirt roads, they drove slowly the distance to Centerline Road. Rosalie leaned forward and directed Marla through the ruts, watching all the time for Sammy and Ophi to pop up in the middle of the road. "They are really in my head now," Rosalie admitted. "This makes the road ten times longer and the ruts deeper."

Marla was a little surprised at Rosalie's fear. She had seemed so nonchalant earlier. "I couldn't do this without you, so don't go bonkers on us," Marla said. She fretted as she hugged the side of the road, keeping the windows closed against any unwelcome hands that might reach in and wrest her away from the wheel. Even with the windows closed, the squealing of the tires as they rumbled over ruts and the clanging of the loose muffler resonated through the hole in the back floor. Rosalie bounced in her back seat after one particularly bumpy patch that Marla had been unable to see in the darkness.

"It would help if there was an occasional streetlamp here," suggested Vern.

"When's the last time you saw a street?" Marla

laughed, a release from the tension she was feeling, from the searching through the black forms along the dirt roads, from the constant peering through the dust-covered windshield as she navigated toward what she considered civilization.

Finally, they turned onto Centerline Road, and some of the angst was gone. It helped to be able to see everything in front of them, to not have to worry about what could appear out of the dark shadows. It also was a relief that, banged up as it was, they had a car that Sammy and Ophi would not recognize. Marla rolled down her window and took in the heavy night air. A breeze fanned through the car and lifted their spirits. It carried a freshness. The blending of fragrances from sweet frangipani and flamboyant trees, from mint and fennel growing wild, the heavy scent of mango, the muskiness of aloe and saltiness of the sea formed an irresistible mixture. "It's too bad about Sammy. I'm beginning to like this place more each day."

Marla inhaled deeply and let out the breath as they passed the correctional center. The presence of Sammy entered the car and ruined her pleasant thoughts. Knowing that he was within shouting distance of her made her tense - her hands gripped the wheel more tightly, she clenched her teeth, and she stepped on the gas to escape the fearsome setting. Ophi's snake tattoo seemed to slither across the road in the oncoming headlights.

She saw the spotlight making its arc across the grounds and noticed the watchtowers at the corners of the prison and said, "Let's hope those guards aren't asleep."

Vern added, "It's really incredible that the warden is part of this whole drug scene, if that's what it is." He cradled his arm and shifted in his seat.

They came upon Sunny Isle and the lighting increased dramatically: streetlamps, neon lights of store signboards, more traffic, and lights from Hess Oil, the giant oil refinery along the coast. "It looks like we've reached Vegas," Marla said.

"Except the stakes are higher here," Vern said. "I hope we're winners and the bad guys are the losers."

Marla looked over at him and was surprised to feel a warmth spread through the car. She remembered the appearance of her mother in the hotel room and her skin prickled, hair standing on end. "I think everything's gonna be OK." She smiled and touched his sore arm gently.

"I hope you're right." Vern's eyebrows dipped

into their doubting V and he peered sideways at Marla.

They drove through Christiansted and saw a little of the Saturday night life. Reggae and jazz music sounded from clubs as they passed by the not-so-crowded streets. In the busy season, it would be hard to get through town without practically riding the brake, Rosalie told them, trying to make conversation, but her voice sounded flat. A few locals took their time crossing the street in front of them. One was a woman who pushed a blue baby stroller. "Why would anyone be out in this part of town with a baby?" Marla asked.

"Look again," said Rosalie from the back seat. "She's a bag woman. She's been selling peanuts for years and seems to get enough money to survive. But you can see all her earthly belongings are stacked in that stroller. Underneath the peanuts."

Marla wondered what else was underneath the peanuts. Could she be a drug dealer? Following close behind was a homeless man, his possessions piled in a shopping cart. Marla scanned all the nightwalkers closely to see if Sammy or Ophi was there. She worried that everyone they passed knew who they were and that news would spread that they had been seen riding through downtown

Christiansted. When they passed the section called Time Square, she was sure she saw Ophi standing under the streetlamp. Her heart pounded, and her fear was transparent. She looked at Vern and said, in a trembling voice, "Ophi," as she pointed to the man.

"Babe, that guy didn't even look like him. Calm down," Vern assured her.

"Are you sure?" she asked. Then she wondered if the man was a drug dealer. Now, she thought, everyone I see is a murderer or a drug dealer! Not so long ago, she'd had no thoughts such as these. Get a grip, she told herself.

Rosalie agreed with Vern. "That's a guy they call Stink Ras. If you'd breathed deeply when we went past, you'd know how he got his name." She checked the rearview mirror, catching a last glimpse of the dreadlocked man, his filthy clothes hanging from his skinny frame. The two opinions sank in, easing her tension.

They began the ascent up King Street as they rounded the corner at Time Square. "Is that a police station?" Marla asked.

"The one and same where I have to report on Monday," Vern said.

"I guess our Obeahmen won't be hanging around

here," Marla said. The church was yards away from the police headquarters. She could see the bell tower of St. John's and remembered what Clemma had said, hoping that the voodoo lovers' loathing of all things religious extended a distance from the church, too.

"If local police were in on whatever Edrick was tracking, Raymond and Eulalie didn't recognize any of their names on the list, so we can be pretty sure they really won't be hanging out in this neighborhood, anyway," Rosalie said. "If they escape," she added.

"Thank God for small favors," Vern said.

Marla wasn't so convinced. Just because the Williamses didn't recognize any names, how could Marla be sure they knew all the police at this station? On the other hand, it seemed to her that if Bob from Christiansted knew Rosalie from Frederiksted, why wouldn't Raymond and Eulalie be familiar with the names of policemen? Raymond had a civil servant job and Eulalie was a top education administrator. Surely they would know the local police on both ends of the island. She decided to take it on faith that they were going to a safe haven, as Clemma had said it would be and that Father Ambrose assured them. She was going to let go and let Vern do the worrying, for the time being. This decision buoyed her up, and the weight seemed to momentarily lift from her shoulders.

They drove through the tall wooden gates to the rectory parking lot. A stooped little brown man came out to greet them. Marla's apprehension returned. So much for letting go, she thought. But the man's pleasant face bore the same serenity as Clemma's and she felt ashamed. "I was waiting in my den for you," said Father Ambrose. Welcome to St. John's." He extended his hand to Vern. "Lamar Ambrose," he said and turned to Rosalie and Marla and shook hands with them. "Let me close the gates so no one can see your car."

Marla was relieved that they would be behind closed gates and was grateful that he had thought of it.

"I don't think the guys we're hiding from would recognize the car, but thank you. We'll be safer with it hidden from view," said Rosalie.

"Come in and tell me your story. My wife has brewed up a pot of hibiscus tea and has some fresh coconut cakes she made today." The little man resembled Desmond Tutu with his wire frame glasses and cleric's collar. Marla immediately felt safe in his presence.

He showed them to their rooms, where they deposited their bags and then led them back into the living area. The priest's home surrounded them and took them into his world. Photographs of children, grandchildren, parishioners, friends, and family adorned the bedroom and hallways into the den and spilled over into the living room walls and surfaces of tables, bookshelves, and the mantle over the fireplace. Where there were no pictures of people, there were paintings done by local artists and those from faraway places he had visited or from places where he had received guests. The Barnes Museum had nothing over the "Museum Ambrose," Marla thought.

Rosalie moved from one picture to the next. "You must know every single person on this island," she said. "Not to mention half the people in the world!" She was standing in front of a picture of him and basketball Hall of Famer Walt Frazier. Next to that was a picture of him and his wife with Senator Ted Kennedy.

"Well, we'll have to bring out the camera, Lily, and take a picture of me with the famous Rosalie McGee and her friends," he laughed. They seated themselves in the overstuffed chairs around the carved mahogany table where Lily Ambrose laid the evening snacks. "Now tell me your story," the priest said.

Rosalie began the tale and Marla and Vern took turns adding to it. When they were finished, Father Ambrose said, "You know the police station is just around the corner on Market Street. Tomorrow afternoon, I'll take a little stroll and check up on the prisoners. We've had a number of problems with corruption. The rotten apple always spoils the barrel, so those few have given the police here a bad name. I'm sure this problem exists in Delaware, too," he said, his kind eyes meeting Vern's and Marla's. "You were wise to come here. We haven't had any visits from Obeahmen as long as I've been here, which you see, has been quite a long time." His arms swept the room as he pointed to the many photographs.

Marla reflected on the story they had told Father Ambrose. It was an unbelievable one, a tale she would never have believed if she hadn't lived it herself. She felt safe here, vindicated of any wrongdoing in bringing the ashes to St. Croix, innocent of charges of putting her friends in danger. Father Ambrose's kind eyes and voice delivered the absolution to her that she needed. She felt as if they were truly on hallowed grounds inside this compound.

The next morning the three guests rose early and dressed for church. Lily was in the kitchen when they came downstairs. "We don't eat until after the second service, but I can make you whatever you'd like," she said.

"Just coffee for me," Vern said.

The other two agreed and Marla asked, "Is there a coffee hour after the services?"

"It's an Anglican church, isn't it?" laughed Lily.

Marla looked at her husband and knew that he was already picturing papaya slices, more coconut cakes, and pineapple treats. "You'll eat your way through coffee hour," she said.

As they approached the main doors of the church, Marla imagined Clemma being here two or three years ago, peeking out at the hurricane. She paused and looked down King Street, saw the sea, and thought of how the winds were so powerful to carry her handbag to the water, thought about the little box on its voyage to Fenwick Island. She and Vern exchanged glances and she knew he was visualizing the same images.

Marla was at peace here, where the chest of ashes had begun its trip. She would have slept through the night, Sammy and Ophi notwithstanding, but she remembered Vern's tossing and turning, noticed the dark circles under his eyes, and knew he wouldn't be content until the thugs were locked up in a more secure place. Rosalie seemed to fit in as though this were her church, as though she came here every Sunday. The bright morning sky complemented her crisp yellow sundress and her smile matched the warmth of the unfolding day. Rosalie's face showed a question as they entered, a question that Vern answered by pointing to the last pew in the church, one by the rear door.

Most people entered through the side doors that ran parallel to King Street, but Marla's anxiety surfaced as she realized Vern chose this spot so he could watch the crowd. All the doors to the church were open to allow air to circulate through the massive building, constructed in the manner of the great European cathedrals. Marla thought of her mother and how she would have loved St. John's, may even have mistaken it as Roman Catholic. The procession that formed at the back door soothed her a bit as she remembered Father Ambrose and his promise that they would be safe here. But a little fear crept back as she scanned the crowd and saw that there was only a handful of white parishioners, that no matter where they sat, they could easily be picked out.

The organ sounded a Bach prelude. Then came the processional hymn and everyone stood, belting out the strains of "A Mighty Fortress is our God." The crucifer led the procession from the narthex at the back of the church to the sanctuary, followed by the choir in their angelic robes, the acolytes, the readers, and, last, Father Ambrose. Their congenial host seemed to shimmer at the end of the procession. The cross was locked into place, acolytes standing at the ready, choir in the chancel, and the readers robed and alert. Father Ambrose lifted his arms heavenward and said, "The Lord be with you." The mass had begun.

Marla noticed Vern looking around the church. She was sure he wasn't enjoying the stained glass windows, the carved statues, the winged angels guarding the baptismal font. She could tell by the straining of his eyes, his intense focus, that he was looking for Sammy and Ophi as he surveyed the congregation. She, on the other hand, examined the bright panels of the window over the altar, the bigger-than-life statues of the Virgin to the right and St. Francis of Assisi to the left of the altar. She ran her hands across the front of the mahogany pew and wondered if Edrick had carved the graceful fleur-de-lis that capped the ends of all the pews.

All eyes were on Father Ambrose and all ears seemed to listen raptly throughout the service. At the end, he asked if there were any new visitors to the church, a common practice at St. John's. He had advised them the night before to not raise their hands, so they sat, feeling eyes on them as the regulars knew they were new. Marla was glad they were in the last pew. However, a few members of the congregation turned in their seats and stared, waiting for them to raise their hands. Marla looked down at her lap, Vern smiled a weak smile, and Rosalie nodded her head toward a woman sitting in front of them. They would have to beg shyness after the service as many parishioners came to greet them. "We don't like to bring attention on ourselves," Marla explained for the fourth time. Several congregants knew Rosalie, but she lied that she had attended a few times previously and didn't consider herself a new visitor.

Sammy and Ophi were nowhere to be seen, so Vern enjoyed himself at the coffee hour and sought out homebaked treats and fresh fruit.

They went back to the rectory with Lily and decided to remain there until they found out whether or not their enemies were still locked up securely. Marla remembered that Father Ambrose said he'd check at the police station after the service. While the cook prepared lunch for the Ambroses and their guests, Marla scanned the books on the priest's shelves. She found a reference book on Obeah and leafed through the pages. "Look at this, Vern," she called. Together they examined the entry on Ophioneus. "Could this be where our dear Ophi got his name?" They read of the water serpent who guarded a living flame in ancient times. "Maybe his job is to guard Sammy." Marla pictured the serpent that ran down Ophi's arm and shuddered.

"Let's see if we can find the source of Sammy's name in this book," said Vern. They looked through the index and found a "Samedi" entry. "That might be a good start. Let's check it out."

Marla turned to the page where they found a lengthy article on the Baron Samedi. "Well this sure doesn't look like our local thug," Rosalie said, coming into the room and looking over Marla's shoulder. Marla was seated at Father Ambrose's mahogany desk, the book lying open in front of her. Vern had pulled a Chippendale chair next to her and leaned forward on its striped upholstered seat.

All three pored at the pictured of a character wearing a black hat, tuxedo, and dark glasses. Something protruded from his nostrils that resembled cotton cigarettes.

Reading through the article, Marla pointed out one similarity. "The Baron had a fondness for tobacco and rum." Sammy had smelled of rum that night at Ohna's and Marla remembered the cigarette dangling from his mouth as he shot pool.

"Here's another feature that I hope is not like our Sammy," said Vern. He read aloud the portion where the Baron was seen only on Saturday after the sun had set, honoring his name which meant "Saturday" in French. "If he escaped last night, he might have played his 'Baron Samedi card'."

They continued reading through the book until they heard the front door open. Father Ambrose came into the den and greeted them. "I see you've found a book that interests you," he said. He explained he liked to keep up with the "pop culture" and had an entire collection of Caribbean practices, history, cults, and the ethnic backgrounds of the many cultures that existed side by side on St. Croix. "It's an interesting mix we have here. Everything from the heart of Africa to the Middle East to the Great China Wall and the usual European population. For the most part, everyone gets along well. A study could be made and taken to the UN to show how harmoniously people can dwell together."

Vern thumbed back to the picture of Baron Samedi. "How about getting along with characters like this?"

Father Ambrose stood next to Marla, considered the article and his answer and resumed, "Unfortunately, there are those who fear Obeah and Black Magic. It's a tradition that's hard to overcome. That's where I come in, along with all the other clerics on island. We fight these beliefs constantly, but a small faction is still frightened to death – sometimes, literally – of those who profess to be spirits." He walked over to the bookshelf and waved his arm at the row that had held that book. "This shelf is full of their myths, fears, superstitions. It's hard to undo generations of these beliefs, but I try – *we* try." His voice trailed off.

"Do you think Sammy and Ophi took on Obeah names to bolster their images?" asked Marla.

"Possibly," said the priest. He smiled at Marla. She imagined that he had been refreshed by her question, that this was something he could answer without bearing the weight of trying to bring people to forsake their cults. "I'm not sure what their baptismal or legal names are. Samuel's pretty common here, but Ophi is quite unusual." He looked more closely at the entry for the Baron. "If this is our Crucian Sammy, he might not know one of the Baron's functions can be a healing one. This character determines who lives and dies. If Sammy has taken on his name, he's pretty likely to be in charge of the dying ones!"

Like Edrick, Marla thought. And Vern and the divers, almost. Remembering where Father Ambrose had been, she scraped her chair against the hardwood floor and rose, almost bumping into him. "What did you find out at the police station?" she asked, nervousness showing in her voice.

The little priest chuckled softly at her insistence. "I was surprised you didn't all attack me when I first came in. But the book had you occupied." He sobered and adopted a serious manner, the mirth disappearing from his sparkling eyes. "The desk sergeant is a parishioner who works one Sunday a month. Lucky for us, today was his day to work," he began. "I told him that I didn't want anyone to know who was asking, so don't worry that anyone can track you down here." Marla was sure he had seen all three flinch a little at the thought. "He called a source at the prison and asked about the two from the shark attack."

"Is that how they refer to it?" asked Vern.

"It's had everyone's attention. We've never had a recorded shark attack on St. Croix, so it was a sensation." His eyebrows raised and he continued. "There was a documented one on St. Thomas 35 years ago and a suspected one that was never confirmed at Buck Island a few years back, but,

believe me, this caper by Sammy and Ophi got a lot of publicity."

Marla's shoulders tensed and her mouth dried. Much would depend on what he said, and she noticed Rosalie also giving him her rapt attention. Vern faced Father Ambrose and held him in his intense stare.

The priest continued, "The two are in solitary confinement. They say Sammy is still nursing some bruises and cuts. They're not allowed to talk to each other or anyone in the prison. As far as the warden helping them get away, I don't think that will happen. This is too high profile."

Lily Ambrose entered the room, breaking the tension with the invitation to lunch. After the blessing of the table and the passing of the plates, Marla relaxed and launched into her meal with gusto, her appetite suddenly taking over. She glanced at Vern and Rosalie and saw that their forks were making their way to their mouths, too. "I think it's safe to say you've been a guardian angel to us," she said to the priest. She felt her eyes glitter, felt the tears starting to build while the stiffness in her shoulders continued to subside. "I'm happy that Ms. Joseph suggested coming here."

"Any friend of Clemma Joseph is a friend of mine," he said, his serious voice matched by his penetrating stare. "I understand what the return of those ashes meant to her. I'm only too glad to have helped you. God go with you." He met Marla's and Vern's eyes with love and concern. "You're welcome to stay here until you're cleared to leave." Then with a broad smile, he said to Rosalie, "Of course that includes you, too."

A Pretty Vivid Calling Card

They drove back to Rosalie's after she reminded them of her dogs waiting in the courtyard. As they passed Golden Grove, Vern made the sign of the cross and said, "So much for your Black Magic now, you losers!" Marla watched him watching the prison go by, following it with his eyes as they passed and not looking away until she imagined it hurt him to turn his head.

Back at Rosalie's, surrounded by the dogs, the three sat in the atrium, Vern drinking more of Rosalie's inflammation tea while the two women sipped rum punch. A trip to the beach was the plan for the afternoon. But as they sat in the comfortable room picking up the afternoon breeze and enjoying the peace that had come over them since the visit with Father Ambrose, Vern received a phone call. It was Mark Allen, the Delaware State Trooper. He told Vern he had arrived that afternoon and asked about dinner that night. He was staying in Christiansted, so Rosalie suggested Tivoli Gardens, a central location.

Marla's tension built in her shoulders again, the presence of the Trooper reminding her that this was, indeed, a serious case, that Mark Allen was connecting dots that linked murder and drugs to Fenwick Island and St. Croix. She was curious about what he might tell them. How much would he share of the investigation? How might they help bring justice to Edrick? No matter what their role, and whether or not they were able to help convict Sammy and Ophi, she reflected, Clemma had lost her beloved son forever. The ashes she carried about were a small consolation, but one that Marla knew gave her a measure of peace. A faint smile crossed her face at this thought, and Vern pulled a penny from his pocket and placed it on the ceramic table.

Marla reached over and slid the coin into her pocket. "Will this pay for dinner tonight?"

Vern shook his head and thrust his arm out, fending off Oliver, who had raised his shaggy head at the action and was heading straight for Vern. "I guess you'll have to keep your thoughts to yourself, for now," he said and tended to the adoring dog.

That evening they sat at the rail overlooking the town and became acquainted over cocktails for the three friends and iced tea for Mark while light guitar music played in the background. Marla studied Mark as he made small talk about Sussex County, one of the only three counties in Delaware and where all three lived. She detected a Philadelphia accent when he talked about the Caribbean water, which he pronounced "wooder," and when he and Vern touched on the Phillies and "Iggles," the way Philly football fans said the name of the Eagles team. She tuned them out and listened to the guitarist play James Taylor's "Fire and Rain," and thought of Clemma and how she never thought she wouldn't see Edrick again that night when he left Mervyn's house.

Mark's quiet voice brought her back to the conversation and she followed the discussion of his schedule, the meeting with narcotics agents the next day, the anticipated meeting with the two suspects. He didn't look like a narc, she thought. Edrick was perfect for that assignment, but Mark was too formal. Short, neatly trimmed sandy-colored hair. Modulated voice, correct grammar, erect posture. More like a Secret Service Agent, a military officer, or the State Trooper that he was. His muscular neck and torso strained against the casual T-shirt he wore in the tropical heat, and she could imagine him in his light blue Trooper shirt with the Smokey the Bear hat worn by Delaware State Policemen. She could even picture the small hand-gun strapped to his side in its black leather holster and wondered if he had one strapped to his ankle because he surely didn't have one under his T-shirt.

They were interrupted by the guitar player, Jerry, who was taking a break and making his rounds to patrons' tables. One of his dogs, a tall short-haired mongrel, accompanied him. Marla immediately wondered if he had some connection to Sammy and Ophi and was relieved to find he was one of the owners and it was his practice to mingle with the guests. She remembered that Ohna did the same thing and this endeared St. Croix more to her with their friendly ways.

Vern seemed irritated by the intrusion and frowned at the owner, who took the hint and moved on. Even the dog must have realized it because dogs seemed to gravitate to Vern, but this one slid his tail between his legs, glowered at Vern, pulling his lips back over his teeth, and followed Jerry.

Mark followed the owner with his eyes and then probed the tables around them, straining to catch a wayward or curious diner, an ear inclined to overhear their conversation. Marla grasped that although they were in this lovely restaurant surrounded by exotic plants, soothing guitar music, steaming trays and plates of local lobster and other culinary treats, that Mark Allen was on official business and his task involved them and their safety.

Mark spread three photos out on the table, "Watch it! Watch it!" The cries startled Marla, and the group laughed when they realized it was one of the two Tivoli Gardens' parrots. The Trooper showed them pictures the surveillance camera had caught at the murder scene. Marla and Vern recognized the beach area. "That's right between South Bethany and those fancy single houses," Marla said. "Where was the camera placed?" She thought of "Big Brother" and realized she was unaware of such cameras in the beach areas.

"There's a picnic area there. Are you familiar with it?"

Marla said, "We don't go there very often, but I know of the spot."

"Well, the camera is stationed on a post at the end. There's a light and a sign on that post, too, so the camera's not noticeable." Mark laid out three more shots of the group at the beach. They were a bit grainy after the enhancement had been done at the state lab. "We've caught several deals going down at that spot. We didn't really catch the actual murder, just the three of them going in and two leaving. Edrick's body was laid out off to the side." He pointed to a recycling container and showed them the area where Edrick had been located. "They weren't trying to hide the body, that's for sure. A guy found it the next day when he stopped at the site to drop off some trash."

Marla felt a sinking feeling in her stomach. She thought of how that meeting could have taken place as they were returning from Rehoboth or anywhere north of their home, that Edrick may have been murdered as she and Vern laughed and joked in their car. Her mother was probably alive then and may even have been in the car with them on that terrible night, while Edrick's mother sat alone in Wilmington, waiting for her son to return.

"That was right in our back yard. I wonder why we never heard about it, "Vern said. "In Fenwick Island that should have been big news."

"We were trying to keep it low key because of the voodoo implications."

"And you know how nothing ever shows up in the news that might scare away the tourists," Marla added.

Her sarcasm was unmistakable, detected by Rosalie, who spoke then. "It's the same here. The Tourist Bureau doesn't like to let the public know when unspeakable things happen."

Marla knew the news would have been sensational, but she knew it would soon have been forgotten, that the identity of the victim would not have affected anyone in her area and other news would have overtaken the headlines. Only Clemma and her family would bear it in their hearts when they found out, and now his death was her burden to bear with them. She grieved silently for Edrick and especially for his mother.

Mark continued, "Plus, when we fingerprinted him, we knew it was Edrick. We were glad it didn't hit all the news headlines. He died of cyanide poison. We think they all toasted each other in a celebration at the site, but of course Edrick's drink was lethal. Death would have come quickly. A few little Cruzan Rum bottles were in the recycling bin, and one had traces of cyanide in it."

Marla, Vern, and Rosalie exchanged confused looks and focused on Mark to explain. Vern was the first to ask, "What could they have been celebrating?"

"Edrick was working for us," he began. "We think he was arranging a buy between the locals in Delaware and the suppliers from the Caribbean. A meeting had been scheduled with the Delaware Drug Task Force the following week, and we think the two had told him the big dealers were going to meet at that beach turn-off. Of course, we'll never know for sure. The voodoo shenanigans were a red herring, something to throw any investigation off. He knew who several key players were in the drug ring down at the beach area and was set to meet with the narcotics team the week after his death. The list you read was what he had been working on. He was close to pinpointing the number one name behind everything." Mark looked around the restaurant again to see if they had attracted any listeners, but the table where they were seated was in a secure area.

He had arrived there before the others and Marla could see that he had chosen the location wisely, that he had seated himself like the Mafia dons in the gangster movies, where he could see whoever came in. They were in the corner farthest from the entrance and she was sure he had checked everyone who had come up the steps. Diners were chatting, eating, listening to the guitar music, and petting the dogs that wandered around the restaurant, completely oblivious to their conversation. The two resident parrots exchanged heated remarks between each other and patrons.

Mark said, "Some of the names on your list were already known to us, but I'm sure Edrick was going to deliver the others to us at the meeting. These two characters, Sammy and Ophi, we didn't know about. Do you think the pictures show them?"

"Well, it seems Sammy wears that Yankees cap all the time. It sure looks like him," said Vern. Marla and Rosalie stood behind Vern's seat as the three examined the photos.

"And look here," said Marla. "You can see that snake tattoo on Ophi's arm. If you blow that up some more, I'll bet it matches his." The vision of the serpent sent a chill through her in the warm night. She pressed her arms together against her chest and hugged herself. Rosalie reached over and put an arm around her.

"That's a good start," said Mark. "Tomorrow I'll make arrangements to start extradition and take them back to Delaware after I've seen them myself and compared them to the pictures. We also have some forensic evidence from the site. I'll take back DNA samples."

"How was it made to look like a voodoo crime?" asked Rosalie, resettling herself in her chair.

"It was pretty eerie – they dressed Edrick up in a ghastly costume, black hat, tuxedo jacket, and strangest of all, some tubes up his nose."

Marla gasped and looked around at the others. She knew they were remembering the book from Father Ambrose's library.

Mark went on after noting their response. "Pretty weird, huh? Then they sprinkled cornmeal and doused him with seawater - Caribbean, no less, like a baptismal rite. The clothes had spatters all over them. There were small clusters of feathers around the body, mourning doves, a special species found – guess where – on St. Croix. If we hadn't identified him right away, we'd have been convinced it was a cult murder."

"Baron Samedi – Sammy Abramson – he left a pretty vivid calling card," said Vern.

Marla nearly asked to leave the table as the thought haunted her of them tugging at Edrick's lifeless body, arranging the bizarre outfit and performing their sick ceremony around him. She stammered, "I think you'll be able to indict him and his partner for this." She told Mark about the Obeah book. She stopped abruptly. "They won't be going back with us, will they?" The thought of being on a plane with the two sent a fresh fear through her body, a tingling of nerves that made her hands shake.

"No," said Mark. "This will be a drawn out affair – lawyers, extradition, grand jury, all that formal stuff. But we can take a National Guard flight out together on Tuesday. I don't imagine they'll want to keep you here for any reason." He turned to Vern. " If you'd like, I'll go to the police with you tomorrow."

Vern looked as though he would jump across the table and hug Mark. "Would I ever!"

Before leaving, Mark said he'd meet them at the police station. "Can you bring Edrick's hand-written list? That'll make an impact on a jury, to be sure, a voice from beyond linking them to him."

Two Mysterious Deaths

After the interview with the police, Vern and Marla thanked Mark for his presence, which helped expedite matters. Vern just repeated the facts he had given Saturday morning and waited while photocopies were made of his driver's license and passport. They stopped to chat with Bob and the crew members who had been called in to give their accounts again and be given the same talk by the chief, who informed them that they could be called at a later date to testify against the two if needed. But based on the conversation he had had earlier with Mark, he thought the activities in Delaware would make the Virgin Islands charges a moot point, that extradition would surely be granted in this case.

Earlier, Mark and the chief, Lowell James, had compared the mug shots to the crime scene pictures, and both remarked about the similarities. They were sure these two were the ones he was seeking. During their meeting, James put a call through to Golden Grove and talked to the duty officer about collecting DNA samples for Mark to take back and made an appointment for him to interrogate the two men that afternoon.

"OK, our nightmare is over as far as Sammy and Ophi are concerned," said Marla as the others finished and they all gathered in front of the police station. "How about one last get-together with everyone, this time - our treat?"

They reserved the banquet room at the Buccaneer. It was early evening, still warm, the sun low in the sky, pale with broken strands of pink and yellow clouds starting to trail from the west. Marla dressed in her lime dress and stood at the entrance with Vern, greeting the entire cast of characters, as she called them. Rosalie, Bob, and the dive crew were the first to arrive. Next came Evie's parents, who had come from the States to be with her as she recuperated. Everyone stood and cheered as the Williamses appeared with Clemma, carrying her son. The old woman's eyes were alert. She looked like she had drunk from an elixir that had brightened her, improved her gait, smoothed some of the wrinkles. But as she fondled her box of ashes, Marla could see the deep sadness that would never be washed away. She hugged Clemma with a tenderness borne of joy, grief, and understanding that is the bond of those who have lost a loved one.

Father and Lily Ambrose arrived, then Scott

from the Frederiksted dive shop with Diarra, Rosalie's assistant, and her husband. The only missing person was Mark. But they knew he had an appointment at the prison and would be coming along later, so they began their festivities. The State Trooper would tell them of the flight arrangements when he got there. Rosalie had told Marla that she was sure they would all want to be at the airport to give them a send-off.

The evening stretched on. From the banquet room, Marla watched the sky darken, the pastel clouds replaced by first a low gray blanket, then a spreading blackness, dotted by bright stars. She and Vern made the rounds, stopping at each table and lingering with their friends. Everyone seemed to be enjoying the final dinner. Conversation was light and at each table, they asked Vern how his arm was doing. "Rosalie's inflammation tea has done wonders," he told them and joked about hoping he wouldn't get picked up for drugs by taking the tea leaves with him to Delaware.

They were so busy socializing they barely had time to enjoy the appetizers of grilled calamari and conch fritters. They finally went to their own table with Rosalie and the Williamses and ate heartily. After the appetizers, dinner salad with a special rosemary vinaigrette came next, and then the entrees appeared.

Other patrons at the restaurant hesitated as they passed the group, leaning against the plate glass divider, seeming to consider what was on their plates so they might make similar choices. Marla saw one man pointing to the room when his server came to the table and the waitress indicated a line on the menu. The man smiled and Marla could see he was ordering the same item.

Strains of classical guitar music from the lounge adjacent to the main dining room reached her ears and Marla remembered Tivoli Gardens and Mark. She leaned over to Vern and whispered, "I wonder what's keeping Mark." She puckered her brow but didn't seem to have a chance to dwell on the thought as waiters came by and refilled the rum punch glasses and removed plates. They always lingered at Clemma Joseph's seat everytime they passed her and Marla's thoughts turned to Clemma, who, she decided, must be the matriarch of the island. She smiled each time a waiter caressed the woman's shoulder or bowed as he served her.

Rosalie excused herself after eating and moved to the table where Evie's parents were sitting with the dive crew. So like Rosalie, Marla thought, so caring, so interested in others' well-being. The parents smiled and seemed to appreciate her concern. Marla reflected on their last visit with Evie, her worried parents in the room with her. Fortunately, the doctors hoped the re-attachment would hold up and that Evie would be able to regain most of the use of her arm.

The Ambroses seemed right at home, the congenial little man laughing heartily at something Scott said. She pictured the priest with all his dignitary friends and wanted to hug him for giving her and her friends the same attention.

The ponging of the steel drums down in the grotto stirred something deep in Marla. "We really do have to come back here," she said to Vern. The gentle breeze wafted through, bringing to her one of her favorite fragrances, adding to her mood. This time it was the jasmine and frangipani sweetening the air.

They were on the dessert course when Mark finally arrived. Darkness had settled over the island and a full moon cast a wide path across the sea below them. Marla put down her fork and reached for Vern's arm when she saw his haggard face. She and Vern left their seats and went to meet him at the doorway to the banquet room. Her thoughts raced. Had Sammy and Ophi escaped? Did they still have to fear for their safety? Had Mark been in an accident?

"Sammy and Ophi are dead," Mark said, his voice matching the fatigued and dreadful look on his face.

Two more people dead. Marla's knees weakened and she felt she would faint. She had brought so much misery to the island. She recalled the shark attack, Evie's arm, the close call of death to everyone on the dive trip, the terror of being stalked, and now, two more deaths. She reached for Vern and he held her tightly, led her to a chair next to the door, and she sat there, stunned.

The others at the table did not hear the quietly spoken words, but Mark's entrance had slowly gotten the attention of everyone. Marla saw them looking at the trio and noticed Rosalie's look of fear. She stood back up and hoped Rosalie would not come to her aid. The group was waiting for a report on the next steps to be taken in the murder investigation and the flight plans. She knew they would be disappointed when Mark said, "I'm not going to stay for dinner, and please don't announce that news just yet. Just tell everyone I'm sick or something." Marla knew this would be believable for his face told that story.

She and Vern stood together, shielding Mark from the group's focus, and Marla saw Vern groping for the right thing to say. His lips were in a tight line, and she felt his frustrated tension as she lightly touched his good arm. He asked, "Are we all flying back tomorrow? This whole crowd wants to see us off. Can I at least tell them that?"

"I need to stay here for a few more days, but you can leave at noon if you want to go back to Dover Air Force Base." He staggered away from them and gave a weary wave to the gathered group. It wasn't a drunken stagger, just a bone weary loss-of- balance stagger.

Marla and Vern returned to the questioning look of their friends. "Is he OK?" Rosalie asked. "He looked like he'd been given the third degree rather than Sammy and Ophi."

"Yeah, he's pretty stressed," said Vern. "He couldn't talk about his appointment. We're going to call him later. Right now he just wanted to go back to his room. He begged his apologies to everyone."

Bob asked. "Did he give you any info about departure time for tomorrow?"

Marla was happy to let Vern control all the information from Mark. This was another of those attributes that she so admired about him, how he could handle any sticky situation. A wave of love washed over her as it had so many times during the trip. She laid a hand on his uninjured arm as he told them all of the flight plans.

A Get-Out-of-Jail-Free Card

On the way back to Rosalie's, Vern called Mark to get the details. "How about stopping here at my hotel for a nightcap. It's pretty unbelievable," Mark said.

As they pulled into the parking lot at the Mariner's Reef, Marla wondered whether or not they should be looking for new ghosts. She thought how she should be relieved that Sammy and Ophi were out of their lives now, but she quivered a little as a chill shook her. How could they possibly be dead?

The darkness folded over them as they got out of the car. How far she had come – from a carefree, sunny, late spring day on the beach at Fenwick Island to a black bedeviled island at night. Dark clouds covered the moon, which had shone so brightly a short time before. The gentle trade wind was gone, and the blackness blotted out the familiar shapes she had grown to love – the coconut palms, stone windmills, gingerbread trim on hotel shutters and eaves. Mark's hotel was lit at the reception area and this lifted her spirits. The receptionist called him and pointed the way to his room. Carefully, in single file, they followed the flagstone footpath, lit by floodlights, which was helpful unless one strayed off the slabs.

The cloud covering moved and the moon lit the way for them, much to Marla's relief. She was holding Vern's belt, trailing behind him, but gave it a downward tug as her foot slipped off a stone, and Rosalie, in turn, reached out to Marla when she saw her falter. Mark was standing outside his room and walked toward them just in time to help balance Vern, who had wobbled sideward after Marla's slight tug, his slinged arm working to maintain an upright posture on the stones.

He settled them in his suite. The room was capacious and had a view to Buck Island and the nightlights of Christiansted. At night, the only part of Buck Island that was visible was a flashing brightness at its highest point to warn low-flying aircraft, but Marla marveled at the lights in the town and the full moon again playing on the water. She could pick out WAPA, the power authority on the island, with its extensive electrical display. Farther away, the sky was lit by Hess's giant compound, light and air pollution visible. Rosalie told them that the plant was situated so that the pollution was mostly blown away on the wind currents. Marla was pleased that it didn't interfere with the fragrances of the island.

Mark poured a rum and tonic for the three and refilled his. He told them that he had driven to the prison and signed in, waited for permission to question Sammy and Ophi, and sat in the waiting room. "I heard alarms sounding. Then a few guards rushed toward the main building, guns drawn. I wondered if there was a prison break or riot or something big, for sure." He shook his head. "It was broad daylight. Surely no fools would be trying to escape then. I could see police cars, fire trucks, just about every vehicle on the island outside the waiting room window. The main island police headquarters is next to the prison, so the response time must have been optimal."

Marla saw that his face was not as drawn in as it had been earlier, that perhaps relaxing at his hotel had soothed him a little. Besides that, she was beginning to think the island rum had some curative effects. His voice had regained its tone of police authority. He was in command again, yet she could tell the experience had taken its toll on him by the way he so often shook his head in disbelief while recounting the strange events. He had changed from the formal slacks, white shirt, and tie he had worn to his appointments and was clad in a Mariner's Reef T-shirt, cargo shorts, and a new pair of flipflops he had bought downtown before meeting them at Tivoli Gardens. Even though he looked quite casual, and was allowing himself the privilege of a drink, Marla felt he still had the bearing of an on-duty cop.

Mark stirred his drink with his finger, added a little more rum, and nodded toward the others but they declined. "Next thing I knew two ambulances raced past and down the road toward the hospital."

"And those two were in the ambulances?" asked Vern.

"I suppose. The warden came to me, finally, and took me into his office. He said they were having a recreation break before the questioning session. This was the one hour a day they were released from their rooms and they were out in separate areas."

"Were they found in the rec areas?" Vern asked. Marla could see his detective antennae sprouting out.

"No. They were found in their rooms. The

correction officers who went to get them to bring them to me thought they were asleep." Mark paced, swirling the ice in his drink as he walked. "They were asleep, all right, fast asleep."

The sound of the ice tapping the sides of Mark's glass prompted her to stir hers. She found the action helped dispel a little tension that was asserting itself again as she imagined the two dead men in their solitary cells.

"Some story," said Vern. "When I gave you that list of names over the phone, I didn't go over any of them with you. I wish I had because I wonder if there could have been any intervention had you known about Herman Roberts. Did you discuss the names with the agent in town this morning?"

"No, I had copied them when I was still in Delaware and we had investigators checking them out from that end. Why, what's with Herman Roberts? Isn't he the warden I met today?"

"Well, I take it you didn't know the warden's name was on the list?" Vern shrugged as he told Mark, his voice ending in a question.

Mark looked dazed. "This goes way beyond my authority. First thing in the morning I'll contact the feds. Someone needs to step in and take over this case. The warden told me about how they were found in their rooms when they came back from exercising." He took a deep breath. "He suspects poisoning, that they were given something in the rec area. With that in mind, it won't be a surprise if the cups they used are never found or they'll be so contaminated with prints on them that no one can be implicated in this."

"It won't surprise me if two other bodies showed up at the hospital and our two have made a clean getaway," Vern said. "Either they've been silenced or Herman Roberts has given them a get-out-of-jail-free card."

Marla's brow furrowed in fear and disgust. "Oh, no. Could they still be after us?" She moved from the rattan chair to the terrace door. Outside the waves lapped against the sand and the sea grape leaves rattled their raspy rhythm, brushing the stucco walls of the room. Nothing hinted of sinister wanderings or murderous surveillance, but Marla had the same feeling as the night at Williamses when the dogs raced out of the house.

Vern held her. "Don't you worry your sweet head." He took her by the trembling hand. "Come on out here and let's see if any boogeymen or Obeahmen are looking for us."

Rosalie followed them out of the room onto the

terrace. Apparently Vern's bravado gave him a confidence that she didn't feel. Rosalie looked suspiciously toward the water and toward the sides of the building, and Marla felt she shared her fear. Mark joined them and the two men's ease lessened the fear of the two women.

They sat for a while and listened to the drone of a returning motorboat. They could see the running lights as it neared the marina and heard it reduce speed as it made its way to a berth. "Who knows? That could be a drug smuggler coming in with a late night delivery now," said Mark.

"And spiriting away the two Obeahmen," added Marla.

"Perhaps," said Mark. "But whatever, I don't think you two need to worry anymore about your safety. If they're dead, they can't get you, and if they're alive surely the warden told them the feds are after them, so they won't want to reveal themselves even if they could."

"Doesn't somebody monitor boats like that?" asked Vern.

"Coast Guard should have them in their sights but it's a pretty big sea out there."

"This must be an interesting job," said Vern.

But not for us, thought Marla. She hoped this

was the end for them. "We'll leave the case to you now," she said, "and tomorrow we're out of here!" She lifted her glass first to Vern, then to Mark and Rosalie.

Henry Rohlsen Airport

Tuesday saw a few of the "gang" at the Henry Rohlsen Airport. Bob and the dive crew couldn't be there, nor could Raymond Williams. Clemma arrived with Eulalie and the box of ashes. "I want you to know that I'm going to let my Edrick rest in peace now," Clemma said.

Looking at Clemma, Marla thought back to the day she arrived, the box of ashes hidden in her carry-on where Vern was unaware of its presence, and now, standing under the portico outside the baggage area, the ashes were where they belonged.

She remembered how, on that first day, she saw the conveyor belts moving luggage as they waited for the shuttle bus to the Buccaneer. She had never seen an airport where nearly everything was outside, under covered areas much like carports or drive-thru windows at McDonald's and banks. The check-in counters, welcome booth, entrances to customs offices and departure lounges were all located along the long, canopied walkway. Taxis and cars carrying passengers stopped wherever they pleased and no whistle-happy police shooed them away. The parking lot was yards away from the business area, not miles away as at the major Stateside terminals. Marla felt sad to leave this tiny home away from home, even though she was glad to escape from the drama of the past week.

Eulalie told them Raymond was building a shrine in her garden where they would inter the little vault behind glass. "*Allawe* will be showing, but Mama can open the glass and turn it to see all four sides whenever she wants."

Clemma smiled broadly and went closer to Marla. "Please," she said, "give Edrick your final blessing. It's you who brought him back to me."

Marla held the chest, turned it, felt the inscriptions and whispered a promise to Clemma, which brought tears to the old woman's eyes. She had made a promise to herself that she would become more open and honest with Vern, and that she would be more accepting and responsive to love and forgiveness, lessons she learned from Rosalie and Clemma. And now she was making a promise to this dear woman whose love for her family and deceased son was a classic model, the kind she thought great writers tried to capture in words and sculptors like Michelangelo tried to capture in the *Pieta*. They hugged each other, a long embrace that was shared by Edrick, nestled between them, sealing the promise.

Marla and Vern waved from the top of the portable stairway to the C-130 National Guard jet. They were on their way to Dover Air Force Base. The tiny group was still gathered at the window of the departure room, waving as the air craft sped down the runway. Imagining the rolling hills and bright colors, the swaying palms and stretches of green fields, Marla felt a great sadness along with a sense of enormous relief. She leaned against Vern and squeezed his arm as the jet lifted. Their earplugs were in place as the airframe vibrated through the clouds and sped northward. Only eight seats were bolted into place and much of the cavernous space was empty, their supplies having been left on the island for the Guardsmen and Army Reserves who were stationed on St. Croix. She wanted to tell Vern how strange a flight it was with no windows on the plane but the noise onboard was deafening, so they spent the trip mostly dozing once they got used to the thundering drone. "No movies on this flight," Vern shouted at the beginning of the trip.

"I guess no meal, either," Marla shouted in return.

"And no talking," Vern added.

Between their frequent naps, Marla eyed the pallets strapped onto the bolted tracks of the airframe. She wondered if any of the sealed "OFFICIAL" boxes may have been carrying contraband drugs smuggled onto St. Croix and flown safely in an authorized aircraft to the Delaware connection, if names on Edrick's list may have been involved in just such a transaction. She'd heard how unscrupulous soldiers had hidden drugs in fallen comrades' coffins and transported them to Dover during the Vietnam era and considered that perhaps smugglers had engaged National Guardsmen to stash drugs in these very containers onboard. Could the terror that stalked them on St. Croix follow them back to Delaware? Would this never end?

PART THREE

Home Again in

Fenwick Island

I smell the beach," Vern said as they crossed the Indian River Inlet. Darryl had picked them up at the Dover Air Force Base. "It's great to be home."

"Ditto that," said Marla and she leaned forward to pat his shoulder.

"Ouch!" he cried. Marla had jarred his wounded arm, a grim reminder he was bringing back to the States of their adventure.

Marla took in all the seashore sights as they neared their home. She loved crossing the Inlet bridge, far preferred it to going down Route 113, the alternate course. Here she could see where the Indian River met the Atlantic waters. Enough daylight remained that she could enjoy the surfers riding the breakers, their black wetsuits catching the light as they rode atop the best waves along the Delaware coast. She remembered how her mother told her that in Europe, many of the coastal areas were unpopulated and it was impossible to see the beach areas from highways. But along this stretch, she appreciated the dunes, the tall sea grasses, the clusters of snowy egrets and grey herons. Even when the encroaching buildings obscured the views of the ocean to the left and bay to the right, she loved seeing the blues, grays, and beiges of the elaborate homes, their white framed structures and canopied decks, circular windows reminiscent of harbored ships.

Remembering the fragrances of the Virgin Islands, she inhaled deeply but took in the salty aroma of the coast with its marshes and seaweed. Visions of bougainvillea, hibiscus, palm trees and towering Norfolk pine played back in her mind, but along the seashore area, vinca and petunias of many colors, crepe myrtles with their brilliant pinks and fuschias and the loblolly pines' slender needles and scaly bark dominated the landscape. Marla smiled as she realized that neither was more beautiful, that each had its own brand of breathtaking. She thought of how fortunate her mother had been to witness beauty throughout the world. Perhaps this was a new beginning for Marla; perhaps she would be free now to explore new places. As they drove through Bethany and passed a small beach area on the bayside, its entrance wrested her from her reverie. "Is this the spot where Edrick was killed?" she asked. She leaned toward the window and turned in her seat as they passed the evil location.

"I believe so," said Darryl. "Want to go back?" He slowed the car, ready to make a U-turn.

"Not right now, but we will visit it this week," she said. She thought back to her last moments with Clemma and remembered her promise. The sun was setting, and she was anxious to get home now that they were so close, to see Mo, to settle back in.

They pulled into their parking space, hefted the new suitcase they'd purchased on the island, along with the Cruzan Rum liquor box, and settled into their home. The first thing Marla did was scoop Mo into her arms. She hugged him as she looked out at the Bay. The sunset visible from her place was, she thought, a sight that couldn't be surpassed anywhere. This evening the welcome home sunset glowed like a field of lava, ripples of flame red and charcoal gray bands. "I've missed you," she told the wriggling cat, who squirmed out of her arms and glowered at her.

"Careful, Mo," warned Vern. "I've got a couple of dumpster dog friends who'd gladly run you out of here."

Dejected, Marla pouted and assured Mo that she understood and hoped the cat would quickly forgive her for her absence.

Darryl suggested they open his gift bottle of rum and have a welcome home toast, but Marla invited him instead to dinner that weekend.

"By then I'll be able to make a perfect piña colada," she promised.

"And maybe we'll have some news about the investigation," added Vern.

Oh no, thought Marla, it's not over.

Barney the

Woodworker

Vern went back to work the next week and Marla visited Barney the woodworker. She told him of the trip and all they had discovered.

"A miracle," said Barney. "I'd never have believed it. When you left here, I just shook my head and hoped you at least were having fun trying to track it down. But I never thought you'd find the owner." He polished a miniature oar he was working on, held it up to inspection and turned it over. "And it was Mervyn's brother?"

"Truly unbelievable," Marla agreed. "Mervyn's coming here next week for a visit. I have tons of pictures to give him of his family and a special request." She shared the promise she had whispered to Clemma, and Barney agreed Mervyn could use his shop, that he'd love to see his old apprentice and would be happy to help out.

Juan Luis Hospital

Morgue

Mark lived in an inland town not too far from Marla and Vern. He came to dinner that weekend with Darryl, both arriving at exactly the same time. Marla waved to them from the front deck, smiling at the simultaneous arrival but noting the vast differences between the two. Darryl, tall and thin - gangly, in fact, pulled his graying hair back into a pony tail in contrast to Mark's buzz cut and muscular physique. Both men were dressed casually, Mark preppy in his chino shorts and tab-front polo shirt, Darryl shabby chic in his faded T-shirt and jeans with the pocket lining showing through the threadbare denim. No wonder Darryl can't find a wife, thought Marla. But she believed Mark looked like a good choice for some lucky woman and wondered if he felt his role as a Trooper could be too demanding on a loved one.

"I can't tell you any details of the ongoing investigation, but I do have permission to fill you in on the so-called deaths of Sammy and Ophi," he said.

They were all sitting on the back deck that overlooked the canal behind the townhouse. Pontoon boats were tied to a few docks along the waterway, closer to the Bay access. The gurgling water and soaring pines directly behind Marla and Vern's home provided a pleasant backdrop. Marla was thinking about the equally beautiful surroundings the last time they were with Mark at the Mariner's Reef and they weren't sure whether or not the two were really dead. The words "so-called" rang an alarm.

"The two never arrived at the morgue," Mark said.

Vern leaned against the rail and watched the fountain spray water over the rock dam below. "Where'd they go?" he asked. His matter-of-fact tone surprised Marla, who wanted to shout the same question.

"Nobody knows for sure, but you can bet it was far from the tourists' hotels. Maybe they *were* in the boat at the marina by my hotel that night," said Mark, and Marla remembered the sputtering sound that boat had made and how they had made weak jokes about spiriting away Obeahmen. "When they arrived at the hospital, the attendants left the meat wagons and casually, slowly - you can imagine Crucian time - made their way to the morgue."

Marla could see them navigating the white labyrinth of halls in the basement of Juan Luis Hospital, following the signs to the morgue. She was sure they took their time. "No problem, *mon.* Time, we have plenty of here," she remembered Rosalie telling her that day in Christiansted as she held up the traffic.

Mark continued. "When they presented the papers to the person in charge and had everything cleared, the drivers returned to the ambulances." Mark hesitated to listen to the bellowing bullfrog in the canal. "Imagine their shock when they opened the doors to find their *corpses* had disappeared! If someone had questioned them right then, I don't think they could have spoken."

Marla was astounded. "Where are they now? Can they find us?" Her voice shook as this new possibility surfaced, that maybe they'd want to come after them. Her mind jumped to the fact that they had been in Delaware before on a murder mission.

Vern did not seem as afraid as he was perplexed. "Who pronounced them dead in the first place?"

"It seems they were only comatose, not dead, when they left the prison," Mark explained.

Marla was both frightened and confused. "There's a difference between comatose and dead, isn't there?" Beams of bright moonlight playing between the needles of the pine trees surrounding the complex caught her expression.

Mark must have read the sarcasm on her face and answered, "In the normal world, yes. But as you pointed out when we were on St. Croix, the warden is an important figure in this case. The prison's doctor wasn't on Edrick's list, but we can be pretty sure Herman Roberts influenced his diagnosis. Maybe in their comatose state, they looked dead enough, so no one questioned it."

Vern leaned against the railing and folded his arms. "These guys really don't get it, do they?" he said. "Here they were with the Delaware State Troopers right in their back yard, and they thought they could pull this off?"

"Looks to me like they *did* pull it off," said Darryl, pulling stray hairs into his ponytail. "Well, at least I guess you got their DNA samples."

"We think we did. We took what was on file, but in this case, nothing is certain." Mark drained his piña colada and refused a refill. "I'm driving.

Wouldn't look too good for a Trooper, on or off-duty, to be picked up on a DUI, would it? Besides, there are more eyes on that hotspot across the street from you since we checked out Edrick's list. It may be one of the drop-offs for the contraband coming from the Caribbean and South America. I sure don't want to get picked up by any of the surveillance team and lie that I was eating a Tortuga Rum Cake."

Again, alarms sounded in Marla's head. "Across the street! I always knew that was a sleazy place!" She moved next to Vern at the rail and leaned against him, and he put his arm protectively around her.

Vern was still stuck on the comatose factor. He said, "Back to our corpses. Surely there were guards and other prisoners who saw them being taken out. Didn't anyone say anything?"

Mark paused before answering. "First, the prison code – gotta keep that in mind. Nobody knows nuthin'. The guards reported they were stiffening and weren't breathing."

"Could the guards be in on it, too?" asked Darryl.

"It's entirely possible. The authorities believe someone slipped in some narcotic, and then a timely call was made to alert the guards that they didn't look right. Usually they were pretty peppy after their rec time, never went right to bed. Sammy was known to experiment with a variety of drugs and local herbs as part of his Obeah *shtick*." He looked upstream at a pontoon boat that was slipping into its moor and went on. "I don't know if we'll ever find out the whole truth about this caper that they pulled."

Marla felt pensive. "I remember when we were in the Botanical Gardens that Rosalie told me there were some pretty serious toxic plants, even some that could cause temporary paralysis."

"And you can be pretty sure Sammy practiced that art and knew he could get the results he wanted," said Mark. "If they're not there already, you'll be seeing their pictures on the local Bethany and Selbyville Post Office walls. They'll be running and hiding for a long time." He put his hand on her arm and assured her, "Don't worry."

A Nightmare

That night, lying in bed, Marla sat upright, waking Vern with the motion. "What's the matter, Babe?" he asked.

I just had a nightmare that Sammy and Ophi were across the street at Crabby's. I saw Ophi's snake tattoo and Sammy's Yankees cap plain as if they were right here in this room." She reached for Vern, shaking as she recalled the dream. "If that's a drop-off over there, what's the possibility that they'll land right here in our front yard?"

Vern didn't answer right away, and this intensified her fear. Finally he said, "First of all, if they do show up, they have no idea we live here, so you can be sure they won't be here to get us. They won't want to be anywhere that someone could spot them. Second, once their faces show up on post office walls like Mark said, I'm sure Dopey over there won't want them hanging out in his place, so rest your pretty head and try to dream a different dream." Vern pulled her close and stroked her back, calming her. "Anyway, if we see them, we know who to call and we can be heroes!"

The thought of seeing them and being the ones

to report their whereabouts didn't soothe her, nor did Vern's weak assertion that the thugs couldn't find them, but his protective arms and soothing voice lulled her back to a fitful sleep.

She awoke several more times during the night, but Vern was fast asleep and didn't feel her get out of bed. She checked the sliding glass doors and looked out all the windows each time she prowled through the house. Finally she decided that Mark and Vern were both right. The two escapees would not want to be near them when they knew they could identify them. They were probably in South America or somewhere where they could be anonymous. She slept the remainder of the night on her La-Z-Boy recliner, Mo purring rhythmically on her lap.

Mervyn Joseph

Mervyn arrived on a Friday evening to spend a long weekend with Marla and Vern. "You're a clone," Marla said as she greeted him. "I'm sorry I never met your brother, but from the pictures I saw, I'd swear you were him."

All three Joseph siblings had the same dark chestnut skin, amber eyes, and slender frame. He had only a trace of a West Indian accent, but his manner of speaking was distinctly quiet, as were most of the Islanders. "Yes," he said as they made their way to the living room and seated themselves on the sectional sofa. He saw the photos laid out on the glass-topped table and picked one up. "If you saw some of our baby pictures, you'd be hard-pressed to identify who was who."

Mervyn was pleased with the pictures, especially when Marla told him they were copies, his to keep. The acquainting and small talk, sharing of the pictures, and settling Mervyn into his room were followed by dinner. Then Vern took Mervyn into his computer room, while Marla cleaned up and fretted. She took the tray of after-dinner Milano cookies and coffee onto the deck and coaxed the men away from the new game Vern had lured Mervyn into playing.

The late summer balminess and gurgling of the fountain in the canal belied Marla's edginess and she knew Vern heard the tension in her voice and probably suspected what was coming. Her thoughts were never far from Sammy and Ophi. She still got up several times each night and checked the sliding doors, often slept in the recliner, where Vern would find her in the morning, usually with Mo on her lap. "I remember your sister saying that the murderers tracked Edrick to your home in Wilmington," Marla said.

"Marla," Vern said softly.

"Yes," Mervyn acknowledged. "We don't know how they knew, except we think they were probably on the same plane when she left St. Croix. She would have had no idea she was being followed."

Her hand shaking as she drew her cup away and placed it, clattering on the table, she said, "Do you think they may be watching you now?"

She saw Vern's lips tighten and she knew that he knew she meant, "Do you think they followed you here?" She then noticed Vern's face soften and a slight smile cross his face, watching her as Mervyn answered, "I have no reason to think they'd be watching me. I understand Edrick was a kind of undercover guy, that he was their target. All that voodoo and Obeah nonsense was a cover."

She was not satisfied, so deeply ingrained was her fear. "Then why do you think they were after us?"

Vern then joined in. "Marla's still worried that they may want revenge on us for leading the police to them."

"I don't think they're *that* stupid," Mervyn said. "I've seen their pictures on the Post Office wall up in Wilmington. Are they down here, too?"

Marla seemed a little satisfied by his answer. Her voice had lost its tremor. "They're in all the post offices within twenty miles of here." She saw the surprise on Vern's face. "Yes, "I've checked all of them." But deep inside, she knew she'd be afraid until they were captured and put away for good.

Marla took Mervyn, as planned, to see Barney Saturday morning. "You're a little taller," said Barney as he looked up at Mervyn. "I used to look down at you; now I can't." He walked over to a cabinet and took a carved object from a shelf. "Remember this?" he asked.

Mervyn held the small animal in his hand and

laughed. "A mongoose! You said you never saw one and I carved this for you! You kept it all these years?"

"I bring him out when I see snakes back there in the yard," he said. "Just the thought of this critter sends them slithering away." He set the carving on a windowsill and turned back to Mervyn. "I understand you have a project that's a little more serious than the mongoose. You can use whatever you want and take as much time as you want."

Allawe Forever

A month later Marla and Vern returned to the location where Edrick had been murdered. It was early October and the beach crowds had thinned. The seashore area was quiet, a light breeze fanned the grasses, and they were the only ones there at the small turn-off. They held hands and waited for the others to arrive. Marla had asked the Episcopal priest to bless the site. She knew Clemma would appreciate that, the fact that they were turning the dreadful location to a sacred memorial.

She tugged at Vern as the cars began to arrive. Mark and Darryl were first, leading the car that brought the special guests to the ceremony. Mervyn pulled in behind them. Marla hurried over, pulling Vern with her, barely able to stop before Mervyn opened the passenger door. She clasped her hands at her breast and tears began streaming as Mervyn assisted Clemma Joseph and her box of ashes, which she had brought with her from its pedestal on the garden shrine. Eulalie, Raymond, and Rosalie followed and all exchanged hugs and greetings. The entourage was complete as the priest pulled into the parking lot.

"I've kept my promise," Marla said to Clemma, holding her so tightly that she feared she would hurt her.

"I never had a doubt," the old woman replied, gazing at the memorial for her son.

Prayers were offered for Edrick and his family and then the priest blessed the masterwork Mervyn had created. The cedar cross was four feet tall, but the bottom length was placed in the 18-inch hole, surrounded by cement. The name carved into the cross looked remarkably as though Edrick himself had carved it: *Edrick Joseph* and below it *Allawe forever.* "Mama, there are no mahogany trees here," Mervyn explained, "but cedar is just as popular locally and has that red tinge to it. Edrick would surely carve cedar if he worked here."

Clemma backed up to the edge of the water, keeping her eyes on the cross and the flowers growing around it. "Take a picture, Eulalie, please," she said. "I want to keep this image with me." She addressed Marla, "Where did you get the flowers? They look like giant hibiscus, but I know they're not." She approached them and rubbed the crinkly, broad pink petals between her thumb and fingers.

Marla explained that they had come to the site

the day before and installed the cross and planted the rose mallows. "Hibiscus would never last through the winter, but these are a pretty close second," she said. "If they don't make it through this year, I'll plant new ones next spring," she assured Clemma. "There will always be fresh flowers here. You'll see how close this is to my home after we leave here. I'll bring cut flowers through the winter."

Rosalie joined them at the cross and thanked Marla. "I want you to know," she said, "that we've become family now, that I have these beautiful friends who've become so important to me." She told them how they had been meeting for dinner, how Clemma liked to wander through her garden, how Eulalie stopped in the shop whenever she was in Frederiksted on business.

Marla thought of her mother and how she had compared the two of them so often. She had brought her keepsake heart with her to the ceremony and had held it when the priest blessed Mervyn's cross. It was in her pocket now and she felt its pressure as she stood next to Rosalie. The memory of her mother's appearance at the hotel on St. Croix flooded back. She looked around at the group gathered there and took Rosalie's hands. "I feel the same. My whole life has changed because of all of you."

She watched as Clemma bowed her head and mouthed a silent prayer, then kissed the box. Clemma reached down and fingered the cross, pressing into the letters carved by Mervyn. Her family surrounded her and Marla smiled softly. *Allawe*, she thought. All of us forever, and the rest of the group moved closer to share in that special moment.

As they were leaving, Vern nudged Marla and inclined his head toward Darryl, who was escorting Rosalie into the car with him and Mark. The two sat in the back seat, Mark serving as chauffeur. They were all going to Marla and Vern's and then out to dinner that evening. "Allawe is truly a powerful word." Marla smiled.

"My peace," replied Vern, using the tone Marla remembered hearing Clemma use so often.

Case Closed

In mid-November the weather was still warm enough to spend some time at the beach. The rose mallows continued to put out the vibrant pink petals at Edrick's memorial site, Marla and Vern communicated regularly with their new friends, and life in general was good.

Marla had returned to school and was the center of attention in the faculty room. The word had spread about the ashes, the shark attack, and the Obeahmen. She found herself actually enjoying telling the stories. She hung poster-sized prints of the island photos on her classroom wall and used them as models. Her students produced more vivid works than ever before. Having come out of her shell, she was more certain of her worth, more eager and alive than ever before.

However, even though there were no signs of Sammy or Ophi, she still felt frightened when a strange car would pass her house and the driver would look closely at her number, when no one spoke when she answered the phone, when the wind slapped a branch against the siding on her deck.

They sat at the same place on the beach where it all began and reminisced at what had happened since finding the box of ashes. "Darryl's going to St. Croix over Christmas," Vern said.

Marla had been following the growing relationship, had talked to Rosalie twice since the ceremony and they emailed once a week. "He has a spring in his step now, doesn't he? And he's cleaned himself up a bit, I've noticed." She thought about his new haircut and not-so-shabby clothes he had begun wearing.

Vern's cellphone rang. "Really!" he said. Marla poked him and formed a silent What? with her mouth as her eyes bored into him. "It's Rosalie."

"News about Darryl?" she said.

"No, about Sammy and Ophi." He put a finger to his lips to keep her at bay.

"Tell me. Tell me," she insisted, but he listened intently as the breeze carried some of the conversation away.

"They were doing what?" he yelled, the connection full of static and made worse by the wind.

Marla moved closer, trying to put her ear where she could also hear the conversation.

"The Coast Guard?" he said. "Yes!" His eyebrows

shot up, he looked at Marla and beamed. "We'll call you as soon as we get home. It's not working here so well."

He told her what Rosalie had reported. "Our boys were up to their old tricks again and surfaced off St. Croix where they were transporting drugs from down-island. The Coast Guard flagged them down and as they were about to board, Ophi opened fire on them." Vern shook his head at the audacity. "Well, the Coast Guard responded and – what do you think?"

Marla knitted her brows and blew an irritated breath. "What? What happened?"

He smiled, knowing he had her hooked. "They shot the both of them, and this time they really are dead!"

Marla sank into her chair and smiled deeply. "Case closed," she said. She gripped the sides of the chair, dug her toes into the sand, and squinted at Vern as the midday sun glared overhead. "Finally, they're put away for good." The thoughts of the sleepless nights, being the sentry on the La-Z-Boy, the fear that followed her everywhere – she dug deeper into the sand, burying all the horrors. "Funny, isn't it? It all started here, and now it's ended here."

They were the only ones on the beach and they enjoyed the solitude, the lapping of the waves, the crisp blueness of the autumn sky and billowing clouds, and the good news. Sea gulls and sandpipers splashed and padded in and out of the surf, searching for tasty morsels. Marla noticed a speck on the crest of an oncoming wave. Vern followed her gaze and stood, folded his chair, and gently took Marla's arm. "OK, Babe, time to get home now, don't you think? We need to call Rosalie."

Marla folded her chair, too, watching the speck grow larger, and gathered her belongings. They headed toward the dune and the path to the street. She hesitated and started back, but Vern blocked her path. "Can't I just see what it is?" She knew her eyes begged like a small child's imploring a reluctant parent.

"Marla." Exasperated, Vern dragged her name out. "We can't do this again."

"Maybe it's a piece of driftwood we can put in our garden." She watched the object grow larger and come nearer and thought, Or maybe a plank from a shipwrecked yacht...with a "Help Me" note etched into it.

ABOUT THE AUTHOR

Fran Hasson is the mother of two fine sons and is a retired teacher. She has lived in Pennsylvania, New Jersey, U.S. Virgin Islands, Germany, and now makes Delaware her home. During her off-duty time, Fran has visited over 40 countries and 25 States. She has drawn on her experiences living on St. Croix, and has spun them into an engaging mystery involving a box of ashes that actually did wash up on a Delaware beach. She welcomes any of your comments or stories of your own experiences in the Virgin Islands at allawestx@hotmail.com

Made in United States
Orlando, FL
29 May 2023

33604834R00192